LAST-CHANCE RANGE

Byrd Elkhart looked on the Territory as his private range. To make his point he strung wire across forty miles of it, and ranchers like Shanley, Reese and Bogarth just stood still and took this latest outrage meekly. But a different breed of cat was coming. He was Clay Janner, of Texas, and the scrawny herd he drove had to go through that wire or else.

Books by Dean Owen
in the Linford Western Library:

THE GUNPOINTER
A KILLER'S BARGAIN
LAST-CHANCE RANGE

DEAN OWEN

LAST-CHANCE RANGE

Complete and Unabridged

LINFORD
Leicester

First Linford Edition
published August 1989

British Library CIP Data

Owen, Dean
    Last-chance range.—Large print ed.—
Linford western library
Rn: Dudley Dean McGaughy   I. Title
813'.54[F]

ISBN 0-7089-6723-X

Published by
F. A. Thorpe (Publishing) Ltd.
Anstey, Leicestershire

Set by Rowland Phototypesetting Ltd.
Bury St. Edmunds, Suffolk
Printed and bound in Great Britain by
T. J. Press (Padstow) Ltd., Padstow, Cornwall

1

THE choking dust coated a man's nostrils and dried out his throat. When he spat into the wind he spat mud. Or so it seemed to Clay Janner. He pulled in his grulla at the crest of a ridge and looked ahead at the parched range, knowing he had probably allowed sentiment to shape his destiny—sentiment in a business where such a luxury could not be afforded. He jerked the dirty bandanna from the lower half of his brown face and glanced back at the sixteen hundred head of Chihuahua steers they had brought out of Mexico. Dust rose in a frightening cloud against the sky, a banner that proclaimed the aridity of this vast and lonely land. The steers were edgy, bawling for water.

Clay's eyes narrowed against the harsh sunlight as he saw his big redheaded partner spur up from the herd. Joe Alford looked glum and once again Clay regretted letting the man talk him into this. Just because Alford had not seen his wife in fourteen months . . .

1

"What do we do for water?" Clay asked.

"Must've been a dry year," Alford said worriedly.

"We can dig for it," Clay said. "If we dig deep enough we'll have the whole Pacific Ocean in our laps." He felt temper rise in him, and he wanted to cuss Alford out for jeopardizing their whole venture on this sorry range. But he owed Alford too much for that. If it hadn't been for Joe Alford, Clay would now be lying under the stony parade ground of San Sebastian Prison.

"Guess you wish we'd split the herd at 'Paso," Alford said. "You'd have your half sold by now and—"

"You're my partner, damn it. We'll see this thing through." He slapped Alford on the arm. "If your wife don't like me then we'll talk about splitting the herd."

"She'll like you," Joe Alford said.

Alford was bigger than Clay, older by three years. His long red hair, last cut by a Mexican barber at the prison of San Sebastian, curled against the back of his freckled neck. They had spent many months in the prison and only now was the bronze color returning to their faces. Their desperate gamble to bring a herd out of

Mexico had finally paid off. But now they could lose everything.

Clay flung out a strong brown hand at the trail ahead. "Maybe we'll find grass up there somewhere."

"We'll find grass," Alford said, the worry deeper in his voice now. "I hope we will."

Behind them, ropes popped against cowhide as the six riders they had picked up at the border pushed the cows through a rocky pass. The cattle might be trail-weary but they were primed for running. Yesterday small bunches had broken free and it had taken all the savvy of the two partners and their men to keep the entire herd from bolting.

"I never seen the country this dry," Joe Alford said.

"Let's face facts," Clay said. "If we don't find grass at your place we'll be selling this herd for bones and hide."

"Spade has always got grass!" Alford said.

Clay grunted. Alford talked tough but Clay had seen the big man's inner softness. He wasn't soft fighting a man with his fists. But when it came to guns Alford was something else again. As they kicked their horses up a steep canyon Clay hoped their entrance into this

3

country would be peaceful. If it came to shooting he didn't know how much he could depend on Alford.

"This time tomorrow you'll be shakin' hands with Nina," Alford said, and beat dust from his hat on a heavy thigh.

Clay felt uneasy. According to Alford his wife Nina was a looker. You didn't leave a handsome woman alone for fourteen months, Clay believed, without her getting around. She might welcome Alford home. Again she might not. And it was her ranch.

As Clay waited for the herd to catch up to them he removed his dusty hat to smear a forearm across his moist forehead. He was tall with a Texas solidness about him. The sweat-soaked shirt was tight across the shoulders and revealed the depth of his chest. As his gray eyes studied the gaunt steers toiling up the grade, he thought of Alford's glowing tales of this country. Fatten the Chihuahuas on Spade grass, instead of splitting the herd at the border and going their separate ways. Double their money, Alford said. At the time it had sounded like a good idea. After all, they had been through hell to get this beef. Every dollar they could realize from the sale of the herd had been earned with

4

their own blood, the months in prison with the constant threat of death hanging over their heads.

This wasn't the first time he and Alford had worked together. Seven years ago when both were just past twenty they had worked for the Rail J outfit in West Texas. They had not met again until fourteen months ago, when they started this mad venture that had nearly cost them their lives.

Shortly after noon they ran into a shaggy-haired peddler who had a wagon-load of tinware and two yellow-toothed hounds. When the outfit drew up Clay spurred ahead and warned the man to keep the dogs in hand. A yapping hound at the heels of cattle as tired as theirs could start a stampede.

The man said the dogs would stay with the wagon. He passed a bottle to Clay. It was rotgut but it cut the dust. Alford spurred up and had a pull at the bottle. The peddler sourly commented on the bad times. The drought had pulled down a lot of the little outfits. He said he hadn't taken enough orders the past month to pay for mule feed.

The peddler spat through a gap in his teeth. "Things ain't bad enough. Now the country's about to blow up on account of a forty-mile fence."

Joe Alford looked skeptical. "There ain't enough timber to build a fence that long."

"Who said anything about a wood fence?" the peddler muttered. Then, sure that he had caught the partners' interest, he went on to expand on the story. "It's a new kind of fencin' called 'bobwire.'"

"There's no wire made that'll hold cattle," Clay said.

"Up north a ways there's a fella named Byrd Elkhart who proves you wrong," the peddler said. "He's the one that put up that forty-mile fence—"

"Elkhart!" Joe Alford exclaimed. "He's my neighbor. Wasn't no fence there when I pulled out last year."

The peddler gave the big redheaded Alford a speculative look. And when Alford took a final pull at the bottle, thanked the man and turned his horse back to the herd, the peddler said, "Is that Joe Alford?"

"Yeah," Clay said.

"I figured he must be if he claims to be Elkhart's neighbor. I heard about Alford, all

6

right. Big and redheaded and with a good-lookin' wife—" The peddler broke off.

"What else have you heard?" Clay asked sharply.

"Folks think he's dead. He ain't been seen or heard from since he left for Mexico to get some cattle."

"Then he'll surprise some folks," Clay said.

"His wife mostly. She's aimin' to marry Elkhart."

Clay sat stiffly in his saddle as the peddler drove off, his two big hounds flanking the rear wheels of the wagon.

Clay's apprehension deepened as he rode back to the herd, toiling across the basin under the hot New Mexico sun. It had been a long trail from the rat-infested dungeon at San Sebastian Prison. Now they had cattle and no water and apparently no grass. And on top of that Alford was about to lose his wife. Not that Clay considered that any great blow. A woman who wouldn't wait long enough to make sure her husband was dead before she fell in love with a neighbor wasn't much of a wife.

Through the years Clay had kept his eye open for the right woman for him. So far he hadn't found her. Maybe he was too fiddle-footed to be anchored to one spot. He was nearly thirty now, and ten years back he had decided that aside from this girl he kept looking for, the rest were easily bought. Either with money or the promise to lead a settled life. Like the girl back there in Texas he was going to marry. At the last minute the girl married a widower, twenty years older. But the widower had money.

Since then, with his rugged good looks, Clay had found his pleasure whenever he sought it. And then drifted on.

Now, riding stirrup to stirrup with Joe Alford, Clay felt a premonition of disaster. To Alford a straying wife would be a tragedy. And it could very well throw them into a fight with this Byrd Elkhart who had put up the forty-mile fence. If that happened they stood a good chance of losing their herd.

But it was too late to turn back. They had to get the herd to Spade grass. Providing this ranch of Alford's had any grass.

To the north, the sky had darkened. "Lightning!" Alford yelled. "Maybe it'll mean rain."

"The rain I'll take," Clay said, and watched the mid-afternoon sky for another flash of lightning. "Thunder and lightning could spook this herd."

8

"I'm hoping they're too tired to run, Clay."

"Sometimes it's the weary herds that spook the easiest," Clay said.

He wheeled his dun horse and rode back through the swirling dust to warn each of the six riders to be on the alert. The storm seemed too distant to be much of a threat, but you never could tell. Their last dollar was riding on the hoofs of these steers.

It had been a gamble all the way, starting last year when Monjosa, the Mexican brigand, propositioned Clay to bring him rifles and ammunition in exchange for Mexican cattle. Clay was one of the few Anglos Monjosa would trust. They had met some years back when Clay was trying his hand at mining silver near Chihuahua City. The mining venture did not pay off but his friendship with Monjosa did. When Monjosa started what he termed a revolution he got in touch with Clay about locating rifles and ammunition. Clay managed to find the weapons but lacked the necessary cash to complete the deal.

Discouraged because no one would lend him money, he ran into Joe Alford on the streets of El Paso. He had not seen Alford since they had worked together at the Rail J. On the chance that Alford might know where to raise some money, Clay outlined the proposition. Alford bought the idea with enthusiasm. He had married a girl in New Mexico who had been left a ranch by her father. Certain he could raise the cash, Alford made a hurried trip north.

Inside of two weeks he came back with the money. Pooling their cash, the two partners loaded the rifles and ammunition on pack mules and crossed the border to meet Monjosa. But Monjosa had suffered a bad beating at the hands of the Federals and couldn't keep the rendezvous. With the countryside swarming with Federal troops Clay hid his contraband in a cave. Hardly had this been done than they were taken prisoner and hurried south to the prison of San Sebastian. There the commandant tried to force them to reveal the hiding place of the weapons.

They refused to co-operate. Clay knew that once they revealed the hiding place he and Alford would be shot. They spent many months in the prison. Then, with the revolution finally going his way, Monjosa suddenly attacked the prison to free them. But it might have ended differently had it not been for Joe Alford. As

Monjosa's men hammered at the gates, the officers in the prison decided to kill all prisoners. They started methodically, using their cavalry swords because they were out of ammunition. When they reached the dungeon Clay and Alford fought them off, parrying the sword thrust with three-legged stools, the only furniture in their cell. In the battle Clay took the flat of a saber blade across the top of his head. On his knees, dazed, he saw an officer lunge at him. And Clay could almost feel the officer's naked blade slice through his chest.

But Joe Alford, unmindful of his own danger, stepped between Clay and the officer. Using one of the stools for a shield, he let the point of the saber bury itself into the wooden seat. Then, before the officer could withdraw, Alford smashed him in the face with the stool. The officer went down. Alford beat back two more who were crowding into the cell, and by that time Clay had regained his feet.

Monjosa's men swarmed through the prison. Clay took them to the spot where he had hidden the rifles and ammunition. And Monjosa, according to their agreement, turned over sixteen hundred head of Chihuahua steers.

Clay, knowing Monjosa's generosity might

pale if he suffered reverses, suggested to Alford that they get out of Mexico quick. They got the herd to the border, and hired enough riders to push the herd north to New Mexico. . . .

For an hour lightning played intermittently around the craggy peaks of the Sabers in the distance. They could hear the distant boom of thunder. The storm was getting closer. Clay glanced back at the herd, his nerves tightening.

Suddenly a woman and three riders appeared on the trail ahead. The woman must have ordered the three men to stay behind, for they drew up and she came on alone. At first Clay thought it might be Nina Alford, having learned somehow that her long-missing husband was near home. But as she drew closer he saw that she could not be more than twenty, with blue-black hair pulled back severely from a high forehead. Clay remembered that Alford had said his wife was a blonde.

The girl reined in, staring at the steers coming up through a pass lined with towering sandstone peaks. Then, as Joe Alford came spurring up, her mouth fell open.

"Kate French!" Alford boomed heartily. He moved in close and shook the hand of the stunned girl. "Clay, you remember me tellin' you about Kate."

Clay removed his hat and nodded. During the long months of their imprisonment Alford had often talked of the plucky Kate French who ran the KJ outfit next to Spade. She had ramrodded the place herself, ever since the death of her brother Jonathan some years back.

Kate's dark blue eyes studied Alford's face. "I heard you were dead, Joe," she said in a husky voice.

"Don't look much dead, do I?" Alford laughed.

Kate bit her lip. She was a pretty girl, her face lightly tanned, her small nose turned up. "The least you could have done was let Nina know you were coming home."

"She's his wife," Clay said. "She'll be glad to see him whether she knows he's coming or not." He sensed now, from the girl's worried expression, that the peddler had given him facts, not gossip. Thinking of how much he stood to lose, Clay knew he would have to talk sense to Nina Alford. Make her realize that her future as well as Joe's lay in this herd. They had to get it north to the railroad. But first some meat had to be put on the bones of the gaunt Chihuahuas.

Kate's full mouth tightened a little as she studied Clay. "So you're the gunrunner," she said.

"If Clay was a gunrunner, so was I," Alford put in.

"You've helped to stir up a lot of trouble in Mexico," Kate said.

"The peons need help," Clay said, shrugging. "Maybe Monjosa isn't the answer down there, but it's a start."

"I suppose," Kate said. She leaned her long body forward in the saddle as if to get a better look at Clay, and even in her levis and shirt she was nicely built. "Is it your fault that Joe was away from home so long?" she asked.

"Joe's over twenty-one," Clay said. "He knew what he was doing when he went in with me."

"It wasn't nobody's fault," Alford said. "How'd you know we was comin', Kate?"

"I saw the dust," she explained, still watching Alford worriedly. "I thought it might be a stranger driving a herd north—and not realizing you can't get to the railroad this way any longer."

"What's to stop us?" Alford demanded.

She told them about Byrd Elkhart's forty-mile fence. "Of course it isn't forty miles of barb wire like he claims. But it could be when the fence is finished."

"Forty miles of fence," Alford murmured.

"You should have let Nina know you were coming home," Kate told him. "You really should."

With that she turned her horse, gave Clay a lingering glance, and rode off toward the three riders who waited for her up the trail.

Alford rubbed his heavy jaw. "Guess I should've got a letter to Nina," he admitted. He flushed with embarrassment. "A man that never learned to write is sure hard put, Clay."

Clay squinted at the dust left by Kate French and her riders. It had drifted higher against the darkening sky. "We've got other things to worry about. That storm is getting closer. Can we make Spade tonight?"

"No chance of that," Alford said. "But there's a good holding grounds about two miles north."

Clay rode back to the herd to have a word with Sam Lennox, the man he had appointed segundo for the drive. Lennox was a big loose-jointed Texan with a shock of thick black hair and a spike beard. He was about forty. He knew his business, but when a US marshal had taken supper with them just north of the border, Lennox had stayed quietly in the background.

Clay warned Lennox about the possibility of stampede now that the storm was nearly upon them. "If this herd runs," Clay said, "they'll lose the little flesh still left on their bones."

Lennox nodded. He and Clay understood each other. They were Texans. Lennox turned his horse to pass the word on to the other men.

Within the next few minutes the storm potential increased. Dark clouds scudded across the junipers that crowned ridges on either side of the immense canyon they were crossing. A flare of lightning tightened the flesh at the back of Clay's neck. He saw the Chihuahuas begin to get edgy in the booming thunder that followed an instant later. It began to rain and the men put on their slickers, tense now in the saddle.

Clay knew a moment of relief when the herd cleared the canyon. The steers seemed docile enough as they streamed across a flat stretch of country. But lightning flashed again above a high mesa and the ground trembled. Probably struck a tree, Clay thought. He held his breath, but the herd did not run.

Then a new sound came to him. Turning in the saddle, he peered through the screen of rain and saw a flat-bed wagon coming along the road. A big man wearing a slicker was humped over in the seat, driving a four-horse team through the mud. Piled high on the wagon bed were coils of some kind of wire. As the vehicle approached the sound of wheels squeaking increased. Clay swore under his breath at this driver who hadn't taken time to grease his axles.

Some distance behind the wagon, four riders pulled up to watch the Chihuahuas moving across the flats. But the wagon came on, swaying from its top-heavy load as the wheels dipped into ruts. Already the lead steers had flung up their heads to stare at the wagon.

Clay turned to Joe Alford, who had reined in beside him. "I'll ask 'em to stay put till our cows clear the road."

"Better go slow," Alford said nervously. "That's Byrd Elkhart's outfit."

"Slow, hell," Clay snapped. "Those cows are already half spooked from the lightning."

"Don't get us in no trouble." Alford flung out a big freckled hand to indicate one of the

17

riders beside the wagon. "That's Lon Perry, Elkhart's foreman. A bad man with a gun."

Clay peered at the slender yellow-haired man Alford had indicated. The rider was astride a sorrel horse.

"Don't be so damn gun-shy," Clay said, and then contrition gripped him. After all, Joe Alford had saved him from being run through by a saber blade back at the prison of San Sebastian. "I'll speak to 'em soft," Clay said, and rode toward the group.

Alford shouted for him to come back, but Clay ignored it. He reined in beside the wagon.

"Can you hold up here till we get the herd by?" he asked the big brown-bearded driver. The man nodded and hit the brake.

But the pale-haired Lon Perry came spurring up to wave a gloved hand at the driver. It was his left hand, however. He carried his right hand sling fashion inside the front of his unbuttoned shirt—to keep it dry, Clay supposed; to keep the long, sensitive fingers warm and supple. Perry pulled the ungloved right hand out of his shirt and dropped it to his belt, above the butt of a bone-handled gun.

"Keep movin', Bailey!" Perry shouted at the driver. Then his small, close-set eyes turned to

Clay. "This here is a public road," he announced coldly. Wind stirred the hair which curled out from beneath the brim of his soiled hat.

Clay tried to hold in his temper. He'd met this type before and he'd tamed a few of them. He wasn't going to let this pale-haired man—or anybody for that matter—stand between him and his avowed purpose. He meant to keep these steers at a walk and then fatten them on Spade grass and sell them at the railroad.

"I'm asking you as a favor, friend," Clay said, and saw that the three riders with Perry had spread out.

The brown-bearded Bailey acted scared, but he started up the team again. He glanced anxiously at some of Clay's men, led by Sam Lennox, who were coming up to investigate the trouble. Some of them had drawn rifles from boots. Disaster hung by a slender thread. If a gun crashed now that herd would be running full tilt before the echoes died.

But Lon Perry's sudden howl of laughter eased the tension. Clay turned in his wet saddle to see what had caused this outburst. Lon Perry's slender shoulders were shaking. He threw back his head, guffawing, pointing at Joe Alford.

The big redhead looked worried as he came up. "I'd admire if you'll let us get by, Perry—"

Lon Perry's thin mouth tightened on the laughter. "You shoulda stayed in Mexico," he said.

"I got a right—"

"You comin' home is going to make a lot of people unhappy," Perry went on.

Clay tensed, expecting Perry to say something about Nina Alford and Byrd Elkhart. Things were bad enough without that.

"Won't take us long to get the herd across the road," Alford said lamely.

Perry said, "Elkhart needs this wire for fence. So you're goin' to wait till *we* get by, savvy?"

Big Sam Lennox looked at Clay for a signal, but Clay shook his head. He didn't want shooting; not with the lead steers milling only a dozen yards away from the team pulling the overloaded wagon. Yet he couldn't back down.

Perry had jerked his head at his three men and they spurred toward the wagon, now moving up the road. Clay started after them but Alford grabbed him by the arm. "Don't mix with Perry. He's bad medicine. He'd shoot you dead and then laugh about it."

"He won't do any laughing if he tries it with me," Clay said thinly. He was staring at the coils of wire on the wagon. "Bobwire," the peddler had called it. The barbs told him the rest. Already "barbed wire" had gained a nickname—and provided it didn't rip the hides off of cattle it could change the whole concept of ranching.

Alford said, "Sometimes you talk like a gunfighter, Clay."

"Maybe," Clay said, and gave Alford a reassuring smile.

Then he spurred away, intending to stop that wagon if he had to shoot Lon Perry to do it. But at that moment the right front wheel of the wagon struck a deep rut. The topheavy load shifted. The sudden weight snapped one of the ropes holding the load. The coils of wire came tumbling across the road. One of them bounced crazily, struck a steer on the forelegs. With a bellow the steer whirled, racing to the north. The whole herd plunged after it.

"Stampede!" Clay shouted. But his voice was lost in the roar of hoofs.

As Clay sent his horse at a lunging run he saw

21

the wagon team panic. They wheeled sharply, overturning the wagon. The driver and the rest of the load spilled over.

Skirting the wagon and the wire coils, the herd roared across the road. Cursing his bad luck, Clay tore after them. He caught a glimpse of Lon Perry and his men riding for high ground to escape the stampede. The wagon driver had managed to scramble safely atop some boulders.

Clay kept his horse at a hard run. Riding full tilt through the mud was risky. He saw one of his men go down as the rider's mount stumbled. The horse floundered, then regained its feet. The rider scrambled back into the saddle.

Clay paralleled the racing herd, dodging horns. He had pulled off his slicker. He whipped it over his head, trying to turn the herd. The rain had tapered off—thank God, he thought—but lightning still plagued them. It struck a butte not a hundred yards away and the accompanying roar shook the ground. Clay knew it was useless to try to get the herd milling. He was too short-handed for that.

He waved at his men to ride for it. Those nearest him were already spurring to get out of the way. Sam Lennox lost his hat as he slapped it at the face of a crazed Chihuahua steer. With his black hair flying, Lennox got away from one steer, but another caught his horse on the left flank and tipped it. Knocked off balance, the horse went down, throwing Lennox.

Clay felt a cold numbness along his spine as a thousand-pound steer barely missed trampling Lennox into the mud. Swinging dangerously close to the panicked cattle, Clay kicked a foot out of a stirrup. Lennox caught the empty stirrup and Clay's outstretched right hand. The momentum of the racing horse pulled Lennox up behind Clay. Watching his chance, Clay veered away from the onrushing herd. Then the cattle were gone, flinging mud from their hoofs.

Bitterly Clay watched them. Lennox, pale around his black beard, swung down.

"I won't forget you saved my hide, Clay," Lennox said, shaken. He turned to peer at Alford who was spurring toward them. "If that yellow-livered partner of yours had backed you up this wouldn't have happened."

"Joe's got gun fever. No use holding it against him." Clay reined away. "I'll send a horse back for you, Sam."

He rode to meet Alford. The big redhead said, "Jeez, I'm sorry, Clay, but—"

23

"Let's not cry about it," Clay said. "Let's go get that herd."

Clay peered toward the hills where he had last seen Lon Perry, having an urge to put a bullet in the man. But he could see nothing. To bring a herd all this way from Mexico and have it stampede because of a spilled load of stuff they called bobwire!

Finally the herd began to lose momentum. To the left, Clay caught a glimpse of ranch buildings. The left flank of the spent herd was tight against a corral. Spurring ahead, he tried to outrun them, for a ridge of hills abruptly narrowed the valley and he didn't want the crazy bastards to swerve and smash those buildings to pieces. Already the van of the herd was starting to mill. He felt better when he saw Alford riding recklessly, firing his gun into the air as he helped turn the herd. Clay shook his head, wondering about Alford's makeup: afraid of powder smoke on the one hand, yet willing to risk his neck in a stampede.

When the herd finally halted the men sat their saddles, coated with mud. They looked whipped. From the distance came a final rumble of thunder. The sun peeped out. There had hardly been enough rain to moisten the ground.

A quick count told Clay they had lost at least a dozen steers that had stumbled and been crushed by the others. Sick, disgusted at the needless waste, he went with some of the men to round up the scattered remuda. With a led horse he rode back to where he had left Sam Lennox. The black-bearded Texan rode on after the spooked cattle.

Then, turning his grulla, Clay saw Lon Perry sitting his saddle a short distance down the road. Perry had a leg hooked over the saddle-horn. He was ordering his men to load the spilled wire back on the wagon that had been righted.

When Perry saw Clay approach he unhooked his leg from the saddle-horn, and his small teeth bit down on a cigar.

"You got any complaints?" he said.

"I have complaints," Clay snapped. He saw that Perry's men had looked up from their work to watch him.

A voice in the back of Clay's mind warned, Don't be a fool. You can't fight five men. You want to be buried here? Perry sat stiffly in his saddle. The man appeared tough, capable.

Perry was looking Clay over, seeing the bristle of beard on the lean jaws, the steel in the gray eyes. But mostly he seemed interested in the black-butted .45 that swung at just the right angle from Clay's hip. A gun obviously for use, not show.

Perry seemed to lose a shade of his truculence. "If you got any complaints, you make 'em to Elkhart. He runs this outfit."

"I will," Clay said, and rode off before he did some damn fool thing and got himself shot out of the saddle. His men were far across the flats, holding the herd, and he was here alone. No, he told himself, it wasn't the time for a showdown.

2

HEADING north again Clay reached the cluster of buildings he had seen earlier. There he ran into Kate French. Four dead steers lay at the edge of a smashed corral where they had been caught when the herd swerved across Kate's yard. Beyond the corral, a shed had been overturned.

"This is a working ranch," Kate told him. "I need that corral and shed."

Tired, disheartened, he answered her gruffly. "I'll take care of it."

His tone caused her to stiffen. "You have until tomorrow to make repairs," she said. She stood rigid. He could see the points of her breasts against the front of a cotton shirt. She might be something to look at, he conceded, but he pitied the fool who married such a short-tempered wench. Her face was red with anger, her eyes bright.

"And what if I won't do it tomorrow?" he said.

"You'd better." The tension seemed to run

out of her shoulders. "I'm sorry, but my nerves are on edge. Everything happening at once—" She glanced across the flats at big Joe Alford talking to the crew holding the herd.

"If I had my way," Clay said tiredly, "I'd push this herd north. Montana, maybe. I wish I'd never seen New Mexico."

"Maybe you should leave," she said. "I have a strange feeling that you're going to bring us trouble."

"You've already got trouble." He told her about his run-in with Lon Perry. "What's this forty-mile fence add up to?"

"It means if you want to drive cattle to the railroad at Las Rosas you'll have to go eighty miles out of the way."

"On account of Elkhart's fence?"

Her lips compressed. "His damnable fence. Drive cattle across the Sink and you'll lose a lot. And they'll lose weight, the ones that are left."

He nodded, feeling a grudging admiration. Ordinarily he didn't think much of women who wore men's clothes and tried to run a ranch like a man. But Kate French was too pretty to ignore. "Are you going to drive across

28

the Sink or make a deal with Elkhart?" he asked.

"I don't know."

"A good-looking girl like you ought to be able to deal with a man."

The anger flared back into her eyes. "If I thought you meant that as an insult I'd—"

He waved a hand to cut her off. "I didn't mean it as an insult. Only a compliment."

But she ignored the apology. "I hope you don't try and go through Elkhart's fence. There's been enough warfare in this country—"

"This game is old to me. One big auger like Elkhart trying to freeze out the shirttail crowd like you. Burn houses, run off stock, fire hay, dam up creeks. This time it's a fence."

"You talk just like my brother did," she said, staring down at her clenched hands. And he saw quick tears fill her eyes. She gestured toward a knoll behind the house. "He's buried up there. That's where that kind of talk got him."

"A lot of good men have died," Clay said soberly. "But you still can't sidestep trouble."

Her lips trembled. "Things can be worked out with Byrd Elkhart. But only if some hothead doesn't throw a match into the powder keg."

"I guess you mean I'm that hothead." He shrugged wearily. "It's plain enough you don't have much use for me—"

When he started away she blocked him. A lock of the blue-black hair fell across her high forehead. "It isn't that I have no use for you. I don't even know you. But—well, you talked Joe Alford into running guns to Mexico. And while Joe's been gone, his wife—"

"What about his wife?" Clay asked, hoping to draw her out.

"It's Joe's problem." She turned abruptly toward the house, then looked back over her shoulder. "Joe's the one to work it out. Providing everybody lets him alone."

She hurried on to the house, skirting the dead steers and the overturned shed.

When the steers were bedded down Clay sat by the cookfire, sipping coffee Joe Alford had laced with whisky. All evening Joe Alford seemed torn between eagerness at seeing his wife tomorrow, and apprehension.

"Why don't you ride on ahead," Clay said, "and see her alone." He hoped the fireworks would be over by the time he came up with the herd.

But Alford refused to consider it. "That's one of the reasons I talked you into comin' to New Mexico with me. Instead of splittin' the herd at the border. I—well, I just don't fancy facin' up to Nina alone. I want you with me, Clay. To explain how things has been with us. She'll believe you."

"What makes you so sure?"

"You got a way with the wimmen, Clay."

Clay gave a snort. "So I've noticed," he said, thinking of Kate French.

As he lay in his blankets that night Clay tried to get Kate French out of his mind. How would it be, he asked himself, to put down roots after all these years? Was she the kind of woman he'd been looking for? But he told himself it wasn't time for a woman to put a brand on him yet. He had many things to do. But Kate was a challenge. It would take some doing to get her corraled. But there was nothing like the memory of a girl as pretty as Kate French to savor in the months ahead while he rode new trails. No, when he finally settled down he wanted a pretty, soft female in lace, one he could spoil by giving her all those things women

31

seemed to think were so important. He didn't want a self-assured girl who could ride a horse like a man and boss a crew like a man. No, that sort wasn't what he had in mind for permanence. But as a temporary measure . . .

3

THAT next afternoon Byrd Elkhart drove his buggy over to visit Nina Alford at Spade ranch. When he saw her sitting on the porch in a white dress, he felt an inner excitement. She'd soon be his, and then he would make up for the lost years. She lifted a hand to him as he wheeled the buggy into the yard and pulled in on the shady side of the house. When he tied the team and went to the porch, she offered him her hand.

"Hello, Nina," he said, and kissed her. She was wearing the dress she'd been married in four years ago, Elkhart noticed and it angered him. It made him think of the drifter named Joe Alford who had come to work here at Spade soon after her father died. Elkhart, sure of Nina, thought Alford presented no problem. But the next thing he knew they were married. Since that time he had been consumed by an intense hatred for Joe Alford.

"It was good of you to come, Byrd," Nina said. She was a small, shapely woman. "And

33

thanks for sending those men over to do the whitewashing last week."

"When we get married and combine outfits you won't have to worry about things like whitewashing."

She peered up into his face. "Is it me you want to marry or Spade ranch?" she said, half in jest.

He laughed. "With or without a ranch I'll take you." His voice hardened. "And I'll be good to you," he added, remembering that fourteen months had passed since big, easy-going Joe Alford had ridden out with his and Nina's savings, to meet "an old friend" named Clay Janner.

"Marry me now. Today. We'll drive to town."

She shook her blonde head. "Four more months," she said. "You know what we agreed. By that time Joe will have been gone for a year and a half—"

"He's dead. You know he is."

She closed her eyes. She looked tired. Running a ranch this size with a three-man crew was too big a job for a woman like Nina. Byrd Elkhart could taste his hatred for Alford. "Wait just four more months, Byrd," she urged. And when she saw the quick anger in his yellow-brown eyes, she added, "There's lemonade in the cooler in the kitchen."

He went into the house she had shared with Joe Alford. Well, after he married her he'd take her to his place. And once he had her safe at his Arrow headquarters he'd come here some night and burn this damn house down. He wanted no memory of Joe Alford. Joe Alford had been a dreamer without the guts to make dreams come true.

He poured two glasses of lemonade and took them to the porch. He'd rather have bourbon but these things could be taken care of once he had a ring on Nina's finger. She didn't cotton too much to whisky. Her dad had been a handy man with a bottle. And at times Joe Alford had done his share of drinking at the cantina in Reeder Wells.

As Nina sat sipping her lemonade she said, "Joe's dead. I'm sure of it. But I want to wait the year and a half. This I promised myself, Byrd. You understand?"

"Sure he's dead. You've got Joe's watch in the house, haven't you?"

"Yes, yes, I know. That Mexican brought it. And he claimed he'd taken the watch from Joe's body. And he said Joe had been shot by a firing squad—"

"What more do you want?" he said gruffly, watching her. In a dark, Frisco-tailored suit he looked the part of the most successful rancher in this part of New Mexico. His brown hair lay tight and neat against his skull. At times his yellow-brown eyes seemed hard and dangerous, but now they were soft as he looked at this woman he had loved for so long.

"Your dad wanted us to marry," Elkhart said, and finished the lemonade. He saw her nod. He thought of how he would ride over here to Spade when Nina was just a kid. How he would take her to town and buy her things at the mercantile. There was an understanding between Nina's father and him. In due time Elkhart would marry the girl and Spade would become part of Arrow.

Nina's father set great store by the arrangement. It meant that if something happened to him, his daughter would be taken care of by a powerful, respectable rancher, and not end up as the wife of some shiftless cowboy who would take Spade away from her, or at best send it into bankruptcy. But that very thing had happened. The old man had been dead only a short time when Joe Alford got a job at Spade during one roundup. And the next thing Elkhart knew, they were married.

Suddenly he took her glass from her hands and pulled her out of the porch rocker and held her tight. "Nina, I don't want to wait," he said hoarsely.

She pounded at his big chest with her fists, but his strength was too much. She gave up and leaned against him. "Four months," she said. "Surely you can wait that long."

He stepped away from her, his wide face tight. "Why'd you send for me then?"

"I asked you to ride over here today because—" She bit her lip. "Well, Ardis Bogarth and Emily Shanley were over here the other day. Byrd, those women are worried. Their husbands are getting riled about that fence of yours."

He removed a cheroot from his inside coat pocket, bit off the end and spat it over the porch rail. With a trembling hand he lit the cigar. A diamond ring on his finger caught the sunlight. "And they asked you to use your friendship with me to—"

"Byrd, don't be angry. But is that fence necessary? Really necessary?"

He bit down on the cigar. "Yes. Or I wouldn't be putting it up."

"When there's shooting it's always the wives who pay. Or any woman, for that matter. I'm thinking of Jonathan French. Kate's brother had to die in the last senseless war we had around here. Let's not have another."

"Barbed wire is a blessing for a big outfit like mine," he said carefully, trying to keep the eagerness out of his voice. Barbed wire was a blessing. It was the answer. With barbed wire a man could fence cheaply. He could acquire land and build and keep on building. His pulse hammered as he thought of the possibilities. To own this whole corner of New Mexico. To go to Santa Fe with a wife like Nina and be known as a man of importance. One day to be territorial senator. Maybe governor.

There was no end to what a man could become, if he planned carefully, if he had the right woman. And the right woman was standing here before him. Although he occasionally took women out to Arrow he loved none of them. He didn't *have* to have any of them. After all, he'd watched Nina grow. And blossom. And Joe Alford . . . The cords swelled in his neck.

"Why fence land that's always been open range?"

Nina's voice jerked him rudely back from his hatred of Joe Alford. "I'm the one that's lost stock, Nina. I've let the small outfits use my waterholes when they made their drives across my land. But I'm damn tired of digging out waterholes after their cows have trampled them in. And I'm tired of coming up short tally every roundup."

"You'll turn people against you with that fence."

"I stand on my own two feet! If people like me, fine. If they don't—" He shrugged expressively. This fence talk was no concern of a pretty woman like Nina. He damned the ranchers' wives who had talked her into this foolishness.

"A fence can be cut," Nina said.

"You don't know me very well if you think I'd stand by and let that happen."

"You'd shoot a neighbor because he cut your fence?"

"Or hang him." He removed the cheroot from his mouth and seemed intent on studying the teeth marks in the soggy end. "There won't be trouble. Unless they start it."

Her face went pale. "I wouldn't stand for violence."

He gave the handsome, taut face a quick appraisal. "It would make a difference between us?"

"You can't get away with that fence," she said, evading his question. "Not legally. A good lawyer would see to it that you were forced to tear it down."

"Nobody in this country has got money enough to hire a good lawyer." He was very sure of himself. "Nobody except me."

She ran a trembling hand over her pale hair. "You can't deprive a man of his right-of-way. The basin ranchers have been driving through Horsethief Pass for years."

"It's on my land, Nina." He forced a smile and brushed the heavy revolver under his coat. He had only started wearing a gun after the basin crowd had made their threats about the fence. "I'll do my arguing with a gun."

"And your neighbors will have no chance," she said heatedly. "Against your guns. And your sheriff. And your judge!"

He shrugged a heavy shoulder. He was over six feet tall, solidly built, but his jaws had begun to accumulate the fatty signs of the early forties. "You build political fences, Nina. Call it buying a sheriff and a judge, if you like."

"It's cruel, Byrd."

"I'll buy out any man who wants to sell."

Her gray eyes flashed. "Ardis Bogarth was right, then. She said that's what you're up to. I wouldn't believe that you wanted to force your neighbors to sell. She's got three children. Doesn't that mean anything to you?"

"Yes it does," he said seriously. He threw his cheroot into the yard. "Times have changed in the cattle business. The small outfits can't stand a poor market or a dry year without going under. The big outfits like mine can weather the bad times. I'd be doing the Bogarth family a real favor if I bought them out."

He went on to tell her that if she stopped and thought a moment she would know he was right. This was a day of careful breeding of cattle, of water conservation, of fenced ranges.

"Those men have worked hard for what they have," she said, her voice indicating that she halfway agreed with him about some parts of the argument. True, this wasn't an age for the small rancher. And yet there was the human element. What to do with such men. . . .

"Nobody's worked harder than I have,

Nina," he said. And it was true. He had started here a year before her father founded Spade. He had worked hard but also he had been lucky. He was facing south now, staring at a spiral of dust curling against the blue sky. Riders coming. Probably the three hands she'd let ride to Reeder Wells for a Sunday fling.

He turned abruptly and took her in his arms again. "Nina, I'll put a gate in that fence."

Hope leaped into her eyes. "You're not lying, Byrd?"

He ran a tongue over his lips, for an instant considering his position. In his code a woman had no business mixing in the affairs of men. Therefore if you told her one thing and meant another it was hardly lying. Not as if you lied to a man.

"If I put a gate in that fence there'll be a price," he said. "Marry me in two weeks. I'll have Judge Samuels cut red tape so you can get a divorce on the grounds of desertion."

She put her head against his chest. "I wanted to wait until August." She looked up at him. "This is a promise? About the gate?"

"Sure." Once he married her he would handle his business as he saw fit. As Mrs. Byrd Elkhart she would have no contact at all with the wives of the basin ranchers. He would make sure of that.

"And you'll keep your promise, Byrd? So they won't have to make that awful drive across the Sink in order to reach the railroad?"

"I promise."

"How soon can you see the judge?" she asked. And then she swayed as if she might faint. He put out a hand to steady her. He turned to see what had upset her so. Two riders were just emerging from the cottonwoods beyond the barn. They halted down by the barn and they seemed to be arguing. One of the riders was Joe Alford.

4

CLAY JANNER'S apprehension had deepened that day. Maybe he was out of sorts because he'd had little sleep. A tight guard had had to be maintained on the herd, and all night he had worried about this meeting between Alford and Nina. Ahead through the cottonwoods he could see the mud roof of Alford's 'dobe house. To the left was a bunkhouse and corrals. The fences and outbuildings showed a recent whitewashing.

Joe Alford looked nervous. "Nina's sure kept the place neat," he observed.

Clay couldn't blame his partner for being nervous at the prospect of seeing the wife he had left over a year ago. Clay ran a hand through his stubble of beard. He scowled at his trail-worn gear. According to Alford his wife was a pretty woman, and a pretty woman might not look with favor on Clay Janner in his present condition.

He reined in beside the barn. "You go ahead, Joe."

Clay argued that a man and wife had much to talk over, in private, after fourteen months of separation. But Joe Alford pleaded and Clay reluctantly urged his horse forward.

As they crossed the yard they could see, for the first time, a team and buggy tied on the shady side of the house.

An oath escaped Alford's lips. Clay drew rein beside his partner, who was staring at the porch. Now Clay could see a tawny-haired woman whom he judged to be in her middle twenties. She was as pale as the dress she wore. She had just stepped away from a big angry-looking man.

Alford dismounted and clenched his big fists. He took a few steps toward the porch, then halted. "Nina," he bellowed, "what's Byrd Elkhart doin' here!"

Some of Nina's color had returned to her face. As Byrd Elkhart started angrily down the steps, she caught him by an arm with her two hands. "No, Byrd!" she cried. "I want no trouble!"

Elkhart drew up, glowering out of yellow-brown eyes at the long-lost husband of the woman beside him.

Clay edged away from Joe Alford and put a

hand on his gun. Elkhart caught the movement from a corner of his eye. He stepped away from Nina so he could watch both men.

Nina Alford was toying nervously with a locket that lay in the cleft of her breasts. She said, "So you're really alive, Joe," she murmured, and then suddenly the dazed look Clay had first noticed in her eyes was gone. "It's nice of you to finally come home," she said, and her voice bristled with sarcasm.

Elkhart took command. He was, Clay noted, the type who was used to giving orders and having them obeyed. A big man in a tough business, this Byrd Elkhart.

"We thought you were dead," Elkhart said blandly. "We heard Monjosa got boxed by Federal troops. And that all Americans caught with him were 'dobe walled."

"Don't look much like he was 'dobe walled," Clay said, wondering why Alford didn't pitch Elkhart off the porch on his head.

Nina Alford said, "We even have your watch, Joe. That's what made me so positive you were dead."

"I lost the watch when we was captured," Joe Alford said. "But you hadn't oughta think I was dead just on that account—"

46

"What was I to think?" the woman demanded. "Not a word from you in all this time!"

Alford reddened. He seemed to be groping for the right words. Elkhart stopped glaring at Clay and turned to the woman.

"Nina, just where does his coming back leave us?"

"I—I don't know, Byrd."

"Don't let him stay under the same roof with you, Nina!"

Alford started for him, big fists clenched. Elkhart came down the porch steps. He drew the revolver from beneath his coat. "You got a gun," he said, nodding at the .45 in Alford's holster. "I'll put up my gun and give you a chance to go for yours. But I won't fist fight you. Understand?"

Alford came to a halt, and he went white at sight of the cocked gun in Elkhart's hand. Clay felt sorry for Joe, but he couldn't keep out of it any longer. "You're so anxious to do some shooting, Elkhart," he said. "I'll be glad to accommodate you."

Elkhart's eyes turned ugly and for an instant Clay thought the rancher would let the hammer of the drawn gun come crashing down. But

Nina hurried down the steps to fling herself between them. "No!" she cried, giving Elkhart a little shove. "I won't stand for shooting!"

Slowly Elkhart let down the hammer and holstered the gun, his face still dark with angry blood. Nina stood on tiptoe and whispered something to Elkhart. For a moment there was a stubborn set to the rancher's jaw. Then he shrugged and went to his buggy beside the house.

As he drove up in front of the house he glared at Clay. "Don't ever ask for trouble from me again. Because next time there won't be a woman around to stop me." He nodded curtly to Nina. "I'll be in touch."

Without bothering to look at Joe Alford, he drove out.

Nina Alford still felt weak in the knees as she watched Byrd drive the buggy out of the yard. If only Joe had some of Byrd Elkhart's strength. She could still feel the pressure of Byrd's strong arms around her. She had been all ready to promise to marry him sooner than . . . all ready to . . . and then Joe had returned from the dead. She stood in the yard, wanting to bawl, but fighting tears. She eyed the tall man with the hat on the back of his head. This, then, must be Clay Janner. The gun runner. My, what a thoroughly rakish, disreputable figure he cut. Dirty. He hadn't had a shave in two weeks or more. But something about the way he looked at her sent a faint tremor along her nerves. Two strong men had faced each other in this yard—Clay Janner and Byrd—and if she hadn't interfered one of them might now be lying dead. Would she weep if the dead one was Byrd? She didn't know. Did she really love Byrd? Or was she just tired of struggling alone? And did she really need a man—really need him? She knew the answer to that. She rubbed her arms where Byrd had held her.

"Come into the house and I'll fix you something to eat," she said, climbing the steps. She lifted her skirts to ease her way, and when she reached the porch she saw that Clay Janner was watching her ankles. A little flustered and at the same time indignant, she dropped her skirts.

"You stick around, Joe," Clay Janner said. "I'll get back to the herd." He bobbed his head at Nina, then got his horse and rode out.

She watched him from the front window. There was a man who knew what he wanted. She dreaded to think what would happen if he

49

stayed too long in this country. If he and Byrd should tangle . . . She wouldn't allow herself to think of it.

Later, after cooking Joe a meal, she sat at the table in the kitchen, watching him eat. Since Clay had pulled out Joe had only made small talk. She wondered if Joe realized he was eating the chicken dinner she had planned for Byrd Elkhart.

When Joe finished eating he leaned back and fashioned a cigarette. "Don't be mad at me," he said tentatively. He told her about the herd of Chihuahua steers. When she seemed unimpressed, he gave her an angry look. "It's bad enough comin' home and findin' a man with his arm around you! But Byrd Elkhart! It's too much for a man to swallow!"

"You swallowed it," she said quietly.

"Damn it, Nina—"

"Don't swear at me," she said, but even as she snapped at Joe she wondered if ever again a man could touch her the way he had at first. She remembered the day he had ridden in here, a big laughing redhead, and how quickly her grief at the passing of her father had seemed to vanish. She forgot that she was promised by Byrd Elkhart, forgot that her father had said almost with his dying breath that he was content to go, knowing she would be safe as Elkhart's wife. But she had held off marrying Byrd. Held off, waiting for someone.

And then Joe had come, and she knew it was what she had been waiting for. But soon she learned about Joe's weakness. He was not a coward; that much she knew. Once, when he took her shopping in Reeder Wells, two drunken line riders had said an insulting thing to her as she sat in the buckboard waiting for Joe. Joe had overheard the remark and beat them both, even though they were big men. So he wasn't really a coward.

But then the talk had started. Bits of gossip to the effect that Joe was gun shy. A card sharp had made Joe back down in the cantina one night by flourishing a derringer. And from then on any man who wanted to see Joe back down would show him a gun. And Joe backed. Not that she wanted a gunfighter for a husband. But in this country a man had to stand up for himself and sometimes he had to do it with a gun.

Soon Joe quit wearing a gun altogether. He started drinking, and he said once that he was tired of being married to a woman who owned a ranch. She offered to put the ranch in Joe's name, but he wouldn't have it that way. "I'll make my own money, by God," he had shouted at her drunkenly, "and buy me a half interest in Spade."

Then he had gone down to 'Paso to buy some horses, and there he had run into his old friend Clay Janner. He had come home with glowing tales of the gun-running deal of Janner's. He asked for a loan. It was to be perfectly legal, Joe said. He made his X on a note and got two witnesses. Then he rode out again, so confident that he would return with enough money to set himself up as her equal.

And now he was back. She felt a moment of pity for him. He seemed so forlorn. And he had backed down in front of Byrd and in front of Clay Janner. She knew the humiliation he suffered.

"Joe, why didn't you send word?" she said softly.

"You know I can't write."

"Janner could have written for you."

"I—well, it ain't an easy thing for a man to admit."

"It wasn't easy for me either, Joe." The moment was gone and now she viewed him

52

objectively. Just a big, good-natured—at least he had been good-natured—uneducated cowhand. Handsome in a way. She turned in her chair and looked down the hall toward the bedroom she had shared that first night with him. Her heart began to pound, but she got control of herself. "I was a woman living alone, Joe. I—I had to fire the old crew. Too many of them wanted to take your place."

"Looks like Elkhart done that." He glared across the table at her. "If I thought he—"

"If you thought he what, Joe?"

"I'd kill him, Nina. As sure as hell I'd kill him if he touched you!"

"Kill him with what? Words?"

He flushed.

"Who did your gunfighting for you in Mexico? Clay Janner?"

"I hate guns!" he shouted. "I've always hated 'em!"

His vehemence startled her and the wave of pity engulfed her again. "Joe, I—"

He got up from the table. "I sweat blood for them cows out there, Nina," he said, his voice shaking. "I damn near died. And I come home—" He leaned over and gripped her suddenly by the shoulder. His fingers dug into her flesh and pain brought a startled gasp from her lips. "Did you let Elkhart?" he demanded. "Did you let him?"

She whirled away from him, her face white. She put a chair between them. Her breasts moved with her breathing. "I should have. He asked me enough. And how was it in Mexico? With your girls?"

"There wasn't no girls! We was in prison!" He told her about the prison of San Sebastian.

But she was so furious that she didn't believe him. Her shoulder hurt from his fingers. If only he had the other kind of strength. The inner strength that would make him refuse to take the things he had taken in this country.

She said, "I imagine Janner was quite a hand with the girls. Maybe he taught you a thing or two—"

"Shut up, Nina." He beat a fist against the table. "I'm home. I'm your husband." Hungrily he reached for her, but she skipped lightly out of his reach and ran down the hall to the bedroom. Once in the room she slammed shut the door and bolted it.

She fell across the bed. But strangely she did not weep. She could feel the tears behind her eyes. Her anger and her pity were gone now.

And she tried to analyze her true feelings. Had she ever really loved Joe? Did she love Byrd Elkhart? Before she could answer either of these questions she remembered how Clay Janner had looked at her that day.

She stared up at the rain-marked ceiling. Was she like some women she had heard of—those who could never stay with one man? The female counterparts of fiddle-footed cowhands. The women who drifted. . . . Terror gripped her. And then she did begin to weep.

5

CLAY was helping Sam Lennox stir up sourdough and beans at the cook fire the next morning when Joe Alford rode in. Clay studied the discontent on the big redhead's face. As one of the men took Alford's horse Clay said, "How was the great reunion?"

Alford told him.

"She'll get over it," Clay said, and handed him a cup of black coffee. He could not really blame Nina for her attitude. It was no small thing for a woman to be left alone in country like this.

But Clay had other things on his mind. A black mood persisted, despite his efforts to throw it off. After all the risk and privation, they might still come out of this on the short end. Unless the herd of restless Chihuahuas got a chance to rest up and feed on good grass, they very well might.

Clay studied the big man who was sitting on bootheels, hat on the back of shaggy hair.

"Why're you shy of a gun, Joe?" he asked suddenly.

Joe Alford blew on his tin cup of coffee and scowled over the rim. "You know how I feel about guns. Knowed it for years. How come you ask me now?"

"We may have trouble before we get out of here, Joe. I just figured it was my right to know."

Joe Alford's eyes were bloodshot. He smelled of whisky. From the looks of him Clay figured he must have spent most of the night killing whatever whisky Nina had kept in the house.

"Joe, you've worn a gun ever since we worked together back in Texas. But I never saw you shoot anything. Not even a jackrabbit."

"I hate guns."

"Why?"

Alford took a long drink of the coffee and sank from his bootheels to the ground. "I was mebby seven or eight when a neighbor man argued with pa about some horses. This neighbor man shot pa in the guts with a pistol that looked big as my leg, and he shot me and left me for dead so I wouldn't be around to tell. I was there alone with pa. He didn't die easy. Every time a man looks like he's goin' to pull a

57

gun on me I freeze. I see that neighbor man pointin' a gun. And I can feel that bullet hammer into my chest." He broke off, sweating.

Clay thought about it for a moment. "Joe, you've got a cat on your back. I hope you can get rid of it before we maybe have to saw our way through Byrd Elkhart's forty-mile fence."

"I oughta kill Elkhart," Alford said. "And maybe kill Nina. If I thought her and Elkhart—"

"Cut it, Joe," Clay snapped. "Don't ever talk about killing a woman. Just get away from her. That's what I always do."

"Maybe you got the right idea, Clay. Fiddle foot."

"It might not work for you." For some reason the idea of drifting on had lost its appeal. Maybe he was getting old. But no. He knew better. Whenever he closed his eyes he remembered how Kate French had looked. A pretty girl doing a rough man's job.

Determined to put her out of his mind he said, "If you don't make it up with your wife, you could head to Montana with me. I hear there's range up there for the taking."

Joe Alford finished his coffee. He sighed.

"The hell of it is, I'm in love with my wife. I don't want to leave her."

"Then for God's sake fight for her!"

Alford got to his feet, his face flushed. Sam Lennox, just roping out a fresh horse, stopped and gaped at the two partners facing each other so belligerently.

"I'll handle Elkhart," Alford said. "In my own way!"

He caught up his horse and spurred it toward the holding grounds where the herd was grazing on the sparse grass. Sam Lennox reined in his dun beside Clay.

"I sure thought you and him was goin' to tangle," the black-bearded hand said.

"Partners have a habit of yelling at each other." He turned away, regretting that Lennox had overheard the argument. It wouldn't help matters any if the hands knew there was friction between the partners. They'd be loyal only if the employers commanded their respect.

That afternoon they moved the herd into the hills, hoping to find better graze. Even though the grass was poor, it was no worse than the Chihuahuas had been accustomed to in their native Mexico. But it would take a lot of feeding to put tallow on them. And tallow meant dollars.

At supper, Alford lost his truculence. He and Clay discussed plans for driving the herd to the railroad once they were fattened up. He told Alford what Kate French had said about Elkhart's fence forcing the basin ranchers to drive across the Sink in order to reach the nearest shipping point.

Alford swore. "Elkhart always did have big ideas. We'll have a meeting with some of the other boys. We'll figure a way out."

"What's your wife going to say if you're forced to turn against Elkhart?"

"She won't like it, probably." He glanced up from his plate, scowling at Clay. "I don't like you tryin' to say that maybe Nina and Elkhart are sweet on each other."

"Oh, hell, Joe," Clay said wearily, and got to his feet. "If you want to be tough, save it for Elkhart. I've got money in this herd."

"So have I!"

Clay held his temper in check. "Because of your wife I'll let you work out this Elkhart business in your own way," he said coldly. "But you better have some answers before we get ready to ship."

He got his horse and rode to a knoll fringed with junipers. Below he could see their cattle scattered in the brush. A long way from Mexico, he thought. A lot of weary miles. A lot of hours off a man's life back there in that dungeon at San Sebastian. Missing a lot of whisky and a lot of smiles from women. Missing all the good things. And all because of a few head of mangy steers.

Then he knew he was feeling sorry for himself. In the early darkness he turned his horse and rode back to camp.

The next day Kate French sent a man over to remind Clay of the repairs he had promised to make at KJ. Clay silently cursed the girl's impatience, but told the rider he'd take care of the matter. Later that day Clay took Sam Lennox and one of the hands. On the way Lennox jawed about his early freighting days out of Joplin, but Clay barely heard him.

At the KJ ranch Kate greeted him coolly. For the rest of the day he worked with the two men, digging post holes for the corral. When that was done they righted the overturned shed.

Lennox combed dust out of his black beard and gave Kate a long look as she came out of

61

the house. "Now if I was younger," he said, "there's a gal I could marry."

"You'd probably be damned sorry if you did," Clay said, thinking of the tangled affairs of Joe Alford and Nina. He watched Kate approach at a brisk walk. She wore her boy's shirt and levis. Her thick black hair hung down her back in two braids.

She surveyed the repairs grimly, then said, "You've done a good job. Now I'll feed you."

Something about her manner irritated Clay. He said, "We're not range bums, ma'am. We don't do odd jobs for a handout."

He spun on his heel and started for his horse. Lennox and the other man exchanged glances. It had been a long time since they'd sunk tooth in anything but camp grub—and here was the boss turning his back on a good woman-cooked meal. Reluctantly they trailed along.

Clay reached his horse, and then he heard Kate running up. She seemed to be fighting for control. "I'm sorry if I rubbed you the wrong way, but—"

"Forget it."

She swallowed. "What happened when Joe and Nina met?"

He told her. "Joe's good at talk. But not much good at fighting. If it had been me—"

"You'd have shot Elkhart?"

"Probably."

She bit her lip, peering up into his face as if she had never seen it before. "Are you really as tough as you sound?"

"No. Tougher."

"Why are you so hard to get along with?" she demanded.

"You haven't been exactly friendly today."

She lifted her hands, running them along the firm line of her jaws as if trying to think of something to say. "I don't mean to hold anything against you, but—well, you shouldn't have talked Joe into going away with you."

"Joe's over twenty-one. He's old enough to know what he's doing."

"Well, maybe Joe will stay home for a while now."

Clay nodded. "If Nina will give him half a chance he'll settle down now for keeps. That wasn't exactly a picnic we had down in Mexico."

"I'm glad he came home safely," she said. "But we were all so certain he was dead."

"You mean that business about the watch?"

"So you know about it." She looked thoughtful. "Lon Perry ran into a Mexican who had Joe's watch. This Mexican is supposed to have witnessed the execution. Lon Perry sent him to see Nina—"

"That Mexican had damned poor eyesight if he thought Joe got shot," Clay said. "Maybe I'll ask that yellow-haired Perry about it next time we meet."

"Now don't you tangle with him." Worry touched Kate's eyes briefly then was gone. "He's a dangerous man with a gun."

"So I've heard."

"Don't make things any worse than they are," she said.

His brows lifted. "Any worse? How could they be worse? We've got a herd of tired Chihuahuas. Joe Alford's about to go loco wondering whether his wife's going to divorce him." His mouth tightened. "If it was me, maybe I'd just as soon she did."

"Huh," Kate French said. "I guess you don't think much of marriage."

"In this case, no. You've got to admit Nina Alford was having a lot of fun acting like a widow with Elkhart."

"That's hardly a nice thing to say!"

He swung into the saddle. "Everything I say seems to gravel you."

"And I feel the same way about you!" She whirled and hurried across the yard and into the house.

As the door slammed behind her Clay had a faint regret that he had lost his temper. But there was something about her that brought out the worst in his disposition. Being married to a woman like that, he decided, would be the same as joining the Army. It would mean war.

The following day Joe Alford came to their camp to announce that he had received word of a meeting of basin ranchers to be held that afternoon at Reeder Wells.

"The boys want to get together on what to do about Elkhart's fence," the big redhead said morosely.

Leaving Sam Lennox in charge of the herd, Clay climbed his horse and rode with Joe Alford across a rugged mountain trail. From a promontory where pines grew thick among giant boulders, Alford drew up. He pointed at the flats far below, hemmed in by hills east and west and by the towering Sabers to the north.

"That's Division Valley," Alford said. "We

65

used to make our drives through the valley. But now Elkhart's got it blocked off."

"He can't get away with that fence," Clay said, "and he knows it."

"Maybe it's bluff and maybe it ain't," Alford said. He pointed to a strip of land that angled in from the south rim, explaining that this was also hemmed in by the fence. "That's part of Charlie Boyle's Sombrero outfit," Alford said. "It ain't like Charlie to let Elkhart string wire across his land. We got to find out about that."

"We'll find out a lot of things when we get to town," Clay said. When they began riding again Clay asked if Nina had made up with him yet.

Alford beat a big fist against the saddle-horn. "She don't hardly speak to me," he said. "Looks like she's tryin' to make her mind up about somethin'."

"Don't let it worry you," Clay said, trying to brush it off lightly.

"Worry me?" Alford shouted. "Why in hell shouldn't it worry me? If you had a wife and you knowed damn well she was tryin' to make up her mind whether to stick in the saddle with you or climb into Byrd Elkhart's buckboard—"

"You worry too much about women," Clay

said, wishing he hadn't brought the subject up. "We've got a herd to worry about."

He felt very uneasy now. If this business with Alford and his wife wasn't settled it could very well wreck all their plans. Alford was loco enough to get drunk and do some damn fool thing. "You better make up your mind whether you want your wife enough to fight for her," Clay warned. "Don't let her even fool with the idea of going with Elkhart."

"You think I should kill him?" Alford said thinly.

The sarcasm in Alford's voice rankled Clay. "Don't get smart with me," he said, no longer able to hold himself in check. "You haven't been worth a damn since the day you came home. You mope around like you'd lost your last friend. Either make her see things your way or forget her!"

"You didn't answer me," Alford said, turning in the saddle. "If it was your wife would you take a gun and kill Elkhart?"

"He'd stay off my front porch or I'd bury him," Clay said. He shot Alford a sidelong glance. "Before you talk about shooting people, though, you better get rid of that cat on your back."

"You didn't see your old man shot. You didn't get shot yourself when you was only a kid—"

"Damn it, Joe, I know some kids who saw Comanches handle their folks rough. Real rough. And they lived through it. One of 'em was a girl. Don't tell me she had more guts than you've got."

"By God I promise you this! When it comes time to do some cap bustin' I'll be doin' my share!"

"That's what I like to hear," Clay said, and grinned.

To ease the tension further Clay asked how Kate French's brother had died.

"Four years back they figured the railroad was comin' through here," Alford said, and explained that this had brought in land speculators. There had been a pitched battle when the speculators tried to back up their demands for land by importing gunmen. One of those imports had been Lon Perry. In the fight Jonathan French was killed.

"Did Perry kill him?" Clay asked.

"Nobody knows. There was a lot of shootin'."

"Did Elkhart engineer that land grab?"

"No, he was on the other side of the fence. He didn't want them speculators buyin' up no right of way."

"Funny that he'd hire Perry after the trouble around here."

"He claims Perry's a good man." Alford spat on a sotol bush growing beside the trail. "A lot of folks don't like it. But the more they turn against Perry, the more mule-headed Elkhart gets about keepin' him on the payroll." Alford grunted. "The whole railroad fight was stupid. When the smoke cleared up the railroad didn't even come here. They built the line a hundred and twenty miles north."

"And Kate's brother died for nothing," Clay said. Now he could understand some of the girl's bitterness, her aversion to possible trouble.

There was a sameness about Reeder Wells that Clay had observed in many towns over the past years. 'Dobe and stone buildings were strung along either side of the main road. Behind the road on both sides the ground sloped sharply to tree-fringed bluffs. Here on the rise of grounds clung shacks, unpainted for the most part, with rusted tin chimneys tilted at odd angles.

They dismounted in front of a squat 'dobe building with a faded sign above the door: FIERRO'S CANTINA.

It was cool inside. A Mexican was watering the dirt floor. Tobacco smoke clung to the low ceiling. A large flabby Mexican behind the bar held out his hand to Joe Alford.

"We think you are dead," the man said. Alford shook hands with him, then introduced Clay to Juan Fierro.

Fierro set out a bottle of Mexican brandy. He had a wide face, made even wider by enormous spiked mustaches. The brandy warmed Clay. There were no other customers.

Soon the basin ranchers drifted in. They crowded around Joe Alford, wanting to hear about the gun-running episode in Mexico. Alford didn't want to talk about it. No one, Clay noted, made any reference to Alford's wife and Byrd Elkhart.

The three ranchers, Buck Bogarth, Tom Shanley and Leo Reese, took a corner table with Joe and Clay. They had a bottle and drank too much. They seemed tense, and kept watching the swing doors as if expecting Elkhart or Lon Perry to walk in and catch them with their heads together.

"This is a hellish business," Bogarth said sourly. He was beefy, thick-necked. "If it ain't drought, it's a rotten beef market."

These were hard-working, serious men, Clay knew. Their faces were leather-brown from the sun. They were determined men, engaged in one of the most hazardous occupations in the world. They knew it and still they kept on. Mule-stubborn, he guessed you could call them. But now the normal hazards of the cattle-raising business had been increased by Elkhart's damnable fence.

Tom Shanley, tall, gray-headed, broached the subject that was on all their minds. "What about that fence?"

They glumly discussed this new product called barbed wire that had been invented by a man named Glidden back in Illinois.

Buck Bogarth sagged back in his chair. "It means the end of free grass," the rancher said solemnly. He lived with his wife, Ardis, and three children on nine sections south of Division Valley.

"It means the end of us two-bit outfits," Leo Reese said, his words hissing through wide-spaced front teeth.

Tom Shanley shook his gray head. "They say

that if a man improves his stock he can run more head on less acres."

"That's only a theory," Buck Bogarth said with a wave of a square hand. "You been readin' the Breeder's Journal again."

"Let's face it, boys," Leo Reese said. "This country is sick. I got half a mind to try Montana."

Smoking a cigar, Clay sat in a chair tipped against the wall, listening to the men glumly discuss their prospects. His first day in this country had confirmed Reese's statement. The country was sick, no mistake about that. Dry years and a lowering of the water level had raised the odds against a small rancher making it here.

And I was fool enough to let Alford talk me into coming here and fatten those Chihuahuas on Spade grass, Clay thought. What grass?

Well, he was in it now, up to his eyebrows. He was in a box and they were nailing it shut on him.

6

THE discussion at the corner table in Fierro's Cantina grew serious. The whisky flowed and cigar smoke thickened about the overhead reflectors. Clay noted that the bar had filled up. Many of the new customers kept looking at the group at the table as if speculating on the discussion, and Clay recognized two of them as having been with Lon Perry the day of the stampede.

The basin ranchers agreed that after spring roundup they would drive their cattle north to Las Rosas the nearest shipping point, one hundred and twenty miles north.

"And unless we bust through Elkhart's fence," Bogarth said heavily, "we got to add on eighty miles more across the Sink."

"We'll lose beef in the Sink," Leo Reese said. "Them that lives will be gaunted. Elkhart's got us up short."

"Elkhart's got no legal right," Tom Shanley said.

"The only way is to get a lawyer," Bogarth said.

"What do you mean the only way?" Clay snapped. "You can shoot a gun, can't you?"

Bogarth reddened. "My wife ain't forgot when Kate's brother got killed. She won't stand for trouble."

"My wife lays awake nights," Tom Shanley admitted, "worryin' about Lon Perry."

"That's the only reason Elkhart's got Perry on the payroll," Bogarth said. "To throw the fear of God into us."

Joe Alford said, "What about Charlie Boyle letting Elkhart fence off part of his Sombrero spread? And why ain't Charlie here, anyhow?"

"Charlie sold his Sombrero outfit," Bogarth said, "about two months after you left for Mexico. To Elkhart."

"The hell you say!" Alford's reddish brows shot up in surprise. "And I s'pose Elkhart's still got the sheriff in his hind pocket."

"And he's got the pocket buttoned." Bogarth mopped his thick neck with a bandanna. "Bert Lynden don't brush the flies off his beer unless he gets a nod from Elkhart."

"Elkhart spends money to elect him," Tom

Shanley said bitterly, "while we sit on our behinds and let our own man get beat."

"That's why the big outfits always pin us to the fence," Leo Reese said. "We can't agree on nothin'. Not even a sheriff."

They decided to form a pool and it was agreed that Kate French should be asked to join.

"Kate hates trouble worse'n poison," Alford said. "And her joinin' a pool would be the same as spittin' in Elkhart's eye. I don't figure she'll be with us."

There was a clearing of throats then and the men exchanged glances. Bogarth gave Joe Alford a significant nod, but Alford lifted his hands in silent protest. Then Bogarth turned to Clay.

"We heard how you talked up to Lon Perry. If we had a tough man to head our pool we'd stand a chance of—"

Clay shot Alford a glance and saw his partner's look of guilt. "So this is the purpose of the meeting," Clay said. "To get me to face up to Elkhart and Perry."

"Don't get riled, Clay," Alford said worriedly. "We ain't no gunhands. But we figure with you headin' the pool Elkhart will step light."

Clay sank back in his chair. "If I didn't have every peso I've got in the world tied up in that herd I'd tell you all to go to hell." He leaned across the table. "But I'm boxed. If I take my half of the cows and head back for Paso Del Norte I'll sell 'em for tallow. So I've got to get meat on them and drive them to Las Rosas."

"Then you'll take the job?" Bogarth said eagerly.

"It's something you don't decide all of a sudden," Clay said, stalling.

"I figure it this way," Leo Reese said, his words whistling through his teeth. "Have a talk with Elkhart. Maybe you can get some sense in him. Me and the other boys have tried. But we get sore and one word leads to another. You got almost as much to lose as us. Elkhart might back down."

Clay reflected that Elkhart was the type who would recognize a gun, but not a fancy speech. But Reese was right in one thing. He had a lot to lose here if things went against them.

"I'll think it over," he said, without committing himself.

When they were outside getting their horses

Clay looked at Alford's long face. "Cheer up, Joe," he advised. "Bad as it is here it still beats that hole at San Sebastian."

The next day Clay and the six riders got the Chihuahuas spread out over Alford's land, mixing with Spade's herd. Spade's regular herd consisted of some five hundred head. Added to the herd Clay and Alford had brought out of Mexico it meant over two thousand head seeking graze in an area that, under drought conditions, would barely support half that number. Clay was damned if he'd give up now, hopeless as the outlook might be.

That evening as they rode for Spade headquarters, Sam Lennox remarked on Alford's absence during the chore of getting the cows spread out over Spade.

"He's trying to make it up with his wife," Clay said. "It's a full time job." He could hardly blame Lennox for making a sly remark about Alford's apparent lack of interest in the herd.

He told Lennox and the other members of their crew to pick bunks in the bunkhouse where Spade's three regular hands lived.

While he was cleaning his horse's hoofs of clay, checking for stones that could make it go

77

lame, he saw Kate French ride in. He was by
the corral and she didn't notice him. She started
for the house but then she paused to talk to one
of the Spade hands, a man named Russ Hagen.
Clay had never spoken to him. He was a
towering slab of a man, taciturn, small-eyed.
He had a broken nose and his right ear was half
gone. A brawler, Clay had sized him up the first
time he saw him.

When Clay finished his chore Kate was still
talking to Hagen. Clay sauntered up, remembering that Alford had said that Hagen had
been hired after they started their Mexican
venture.

Hagen saw him coming, gave him a black
look, then wheeled for the bunkhouse.

"You say something to upset our boy
Hagen?" Clay said.

The sound of his voice brought Kate spinning
around so sharply that her long blue-black
braids whipped across her shoulders. She said,
"Hagen used to work for Elkhart before Nina
hired him. I asked him if he thought Elkhart
would back down about the fence. If enough
pressure was put on him, that is."

Clay stared thoughtfully at the bunkhouse
where he could see Hagen watching him from

a window. "Might be interesting to learn why Hagen left Elkhart's payroll and came here," he said softly.

"Don't make an issue out of the simple fact of a rider changing jobs," Kate warned.

"Just seems odd that he'd come over here to work."

Kate's blue eyes clouded angrily. "I guess I was right about you," she said. "You're a trouble maker. You seem to go out of your way to create tension." Her dark hair was pulled back smoothly from her high forehead, and in the growing shadows she seemed quite tall, capable in a gray wool shirt and black riding breeches. "Instead of trying to read some sinister motive in Hagen's working here, why don't you have your talk with Elkhart?"

"What about my talk with Elkhart?" he demanded quietly. Some of the men were heading for the bunkhouse, bedrolls balanced on their shoulders.

"You promised Bogarth and the rest of the basin outfits that you'd try to reason with Elkhart."

"I didn't promise. I told them I'd think it over."

"And when you think it over I suppose you'll

come to the conclusion that a gun is the only answer."

He shrugged. "Maybe."

"You accept failure before you even try. Because it's the way you want it—" Her voice broke. "Sometimes I wish you and Lon Perry would fight it out between you and settle the thing once and for all."

She started to stomp furiously toward the house. He caught her by the wrist and jerked her around. "I know you haven't had it easy, Kate," he said. "And I'm sorry you lost your brother. But don't let it sour your whole life—"

"Let me go!" she screamed, and tried to tear his fingers from her wrist.

But the more she struggled, the tighter he held on. Some of the men were looking at them, surprised.

Then Sam Lennox cried, "Watch it, Clay!"

Clay turned her loose, spun on a heel and saw Russ Hagen lunging for him. And as Hagen came lumbering in, huge fists flailing the air, Clay thought: He's been waiting for a chance to tangle with me. And now he's got it.

But he had no intention of wasting his strength fighting such a formidable man, a man so experienced in rough-and-tumble, if his scars proved anything.

He gave Kate a shove to get her out of the way. Then he jerked aside as Hagen's fist whistled across the spot where his face had been. Off balance as the powerful blow failed to land, Hagen stumbled. Clay struck him behind the right ear with a clubbed fist. Hagen went to his knees. Clay stepped back and drew his gun.

"On your feet," he said.

Hagen got to his feet, glaring.

Kate French stood with a fist at her mouth. She was dead white. Clay ordered Hagen to turn around. He got Hagen's gun and tossed it to Sam Lennox.

"Don't give it back to him till he cools off," Clay ordered.

Lennox grinned through his beard. "Sure, boss. But you oughta clean him good for tryin' to jump you."

"I won't break my fists on his hard head." He eyed Hagen. "You jump me again and you'll get a pound of lead in the gut."

Hagen rubbed the sore spot behind his ear where Clay had clubbed him. "You're scared to fist fight me."

Clay grinned coldly. "Who put you up to this —Elkhart?"

Hagen blinked and Clay knew the truth.

"If you were one of my riders," Clay said, "I'd fire you off the place. But you work for the Alfords. If they want to keep you on it's their business. Just stay out of my way after this."

Swearing under his breath, Hagen lumbered off to the bunkhouse. "*You* better watch out for *him*," Sam Lennox said. "He's a mean one."

Kate French stood in the Spade parlor, trembling with rage. She kept looking down at the red marks on her wrists left by Clay's fingers. "I hate him!" she cried.

Nina Alford's pale brows arched quizzically.

"Hate is a funny thing," she said in her rich voice. "Sometimes it's love in disguise." She glanced through the window. There stood Clay Janner, tall and rugged talking to some of his men.

Kate followed her gaze. "Me in love with *him?*" She gave a shaky laugh.

Nina said, "He handled Russ Hagen neatly. And Hagen is nobody to fool with. He's crippled a couple of men since he's been in this country."

Kate flinched. She flung a hasty glance at the yard, but Clay was gone.

Nina gave her a small smile. "Afraid Hagen might cripple Clay Janner?"

"Of course not. It does seem odd that you'd hire one of Elkhart's former riders."

Nina Alford shrugged. "Hagen had a fight with Byrd. He wanted a job and riders were hard to come by. At least the kind who'd leave me alone." She raised a small hand to touch her pinned-up hair. "It wasn't easy being around men—when they considered me a widow."

"And Elkhart didn't object to Hagen working for you? He's always insisted that any man he fires get out of the country. At least up until now."

"Byrd never interfered with my personal business."

"How are things coming with you and Joe?" Kate asked. "That's why I came over—"

"He's mad because I won't take him back without an argument." Nina sank to a horsehair sofa and smoothed her blue dress. "He went storming out of here a while ago."

"You've got to make up your mind one way or another."

"Byrd sent word today," Nina admitted. "He wants an answer."

"Joe shouldn't have gone off and left you," Kate said. "But, after all, he's still your husband."

"It's Clay Janner's fault," Nina said bitterly. "This whole mess—" Her voice trailed off. Through the window she saw the tall Texan striding toward the corral.

"Let me know how you make out with Joe," Kate said.

"Is the whole country worried about me and my husband?" Nina asked with a faint smile.

"A lot of people seem to think it's important," Kate said. "If you marry Byrd Elkhart they seem to feel you'll have enough influence to get him to tear down that fence."

"He already promised me that—if I marry him." She lost her smile and became serious. "What would you do in my place, Kate?"

"Maybe I'm old-fashioned. But I'd stick with my husband."

"You wouldn't marry a weakling as I did," Nina said. "You would marry a strong man."

"Joe isn't weak. He just—just hasn't found himself."

"I'd like to believe that," Nina said. "But I don't. I feel that Joe is a man who always drifted from job to job. Now that he's faced with responsibilities he can't cope with life."

"You owning a ranch doesn't help Joe's pride."

"It doesn't help my pride any to know that at one time or another most of the people in this country have laughed behind my husband's back."

"Because he won't fight with a gun?" Kate asked.

"He's yellow," Nina said. "I know it and he knows it." She got to her feet, somehow looking older. "One thing I've got to do and that's get Clay Janner away from Spade. As long as he's here there'll be the threat of real trouble."

"That may not be easy."

"Women have a way of doing these things," Nina said. "Anyway, if the burden rests with me I'll have a try at it."

Kate turned for the door. "Does Joe know yet that you really intended to marry Byrd Elkhart?"

"No. And I hope to God he never finds out."

Immediately after Kate left, Joe Alford came from the back part of the house. His face was gray. Nina put both hands over her mouth, and then she lowered them slowly.

"You've been back there," she said. "All this time. Listening."

"I learned a lot of things," he said numbly.

"Joe, I—"

"So I'm yellow."

"I didn't mean that. Not really." She took a step toward him. "But, Joe, why don't you help me? I'm tired of carrying this ranch on my back."

"I've done my share of work."

"For fourteen months you didn't do your share."

"I brung home beef. I got enough to buy a half interest in this ranch. But now I don't give a damn about it. Go ahead and marry Byrd Elkhart."

"Like Kate said, you're still my husband."

"Hah!" He started to leave the room but she ran to the doorway and flung her arms wide and blocked him. "Joe, I'm sorry for the things I said. But you haven't made it easy since you came back. Accusing me—"

"You and Elkhart."

"I swear to you that nothing happened between us."

He shook his shaggy red head. "I don't believe it."

Her mouth became an angry line. "And what were you doing in Mexico?"

"I told you!"

"If you don't believe me, I don't believe you. That story about prison is a lie!" Her voice rose shrilly. "You and Clay Janner in Mexico, having yourselves a time! And me, trying to run this ranch and keep the whole country from blowing up around me!"

Joe Alford just stood woodenly in the doorway. She began to cry.

"Joe, why can't you be strong?"

He flexed a thick arm. "I'm strong as anybody."

"I don't mean that kind of strength." She dashed tears from her eyes with the back of a hand. "Why don't you stand up for yourself?"

"You want me to face up to Lon Perry. That's it, ain't it?"

"I didn't say that—"

"You want Perry to kill me. Then you'll be shut of me for good."

"Joe, that isn't so." She stepped away from

87

him. "Why don't you be Joe Alford's man for a change? Why don't you—take what you want?"

She let her hands fall slowly to her sides. She waited for him. Outside, hoofs rattled against the corral fence as one of the men tried to break a horse.

Joe Alford took a step toward her, then turned on his heel. "Go ahead and get your divorce. You was goin' to marry Elkhart, anyhow."

"Joe, I made the first move," she warned. "Don't turn your back on me."

"Elkhart would own a right nice chunk of this country if he got hold of Spade by marrying you."

He stomped out of the house. She screamed at him to come back, but he didn't. She walked over to the front window and saw Clay Janner sitting on the top rail of the corral fence, watching the horse breaker. She dried her tears.

"All right, Joe," she said under her breath. "You asked for it."

7

CLAY got directions to Elkhart's Arrow spread and set out after breakfast. With the early sun at his back he felt almost at peace. With a little rain this would be good country. A place where a man could put down his roots and get married. . . . He swore softly. This was hardly the time to think about settling down.

Because the forty-mile fence hadn't been finished, Clay was able to reach Arrow headquarters without going through a gate or cutting wire. He skirted a fence-building crew and topped a rise of ground overlooking the spacious barns and main house of Arrow. As he drew nearer he saw that the house was 'dobe with a red-tiled roof. The two barns were huge, the corrals filled with fine horses. Even the blacksmith shop seemed to be in better shape than the main house of most ranches. Beside the house a row of cottonwoods stirred in the breeze. It was a layout to make a man catch his breath. In a way he couldn't blame Nina Alford for toying with the idea of marrying all of this.

Passing the blacksmith shop, he heard somebody yell: "Here comes Janner. Watch it, boys!"

Clay drew rein, dropping a hand to his gun. Three Arrow hands, holding rifles, ran out of the bunkhouse. Three more appeared at the corral, also holding rifles. Clay shifted his gaze. Elkhart had come to the porch of the house, a cigar clenched between his teeth. His big hands gripped the porch rail.

Clay felt the growing tension. He could turn and ride for it, but that would make him out to be a coward. Besides, now that he thought about it, the situation seemed amusing in a way. It appeared that Elkhart was so afraid that he had six men covering him with rifles.

Clay looked at the nearest man, young, bald, with a wedge-shaped face and small glittering eyes. "Welcoming committee?" he asked.

"Keep moving," the bald man ordered.

Clay touched his horse lightly with the spurs and rode on toward the house, passing other groups of armed men who watched him coldly.

As Clay drew rein in front of the veranda Elkhart released his grip on the porch rail but continued to regard his visitor warily. Smoke curled up from his cigar to spread across his broad face. He wore a black suit and white shirt with a string tie.

"All right, you're here," Elkhart said. "Now what?"

Clay swung down. "I came to talk. No other reason."

"Then talk," the rancher said in a strained voice.

Clay narrowed his eyes, wondering at Elkhart's apparent uneasiness. Something was wrong here, but he couldn't for the life of him figure out what it was.

"You act like I'd come riding in here with a gun in each hand," Clay said.

Elkhart's lips barely moved as he murmured, "You said you wanted to talk. Get at it."

The man's blunt manner put a raw resentment in Clay, but he held himself in. Too many others were involved in this mess—Kate, for one. He told Elkhart why he had come: that some of Arrow's neighbors wanted to know what was to be done about the forty-mile fence.

"Why didn't they come themselves," Elkhart said, "instead of sending a stranger?"

"I own a half interest in a herd of cattle,"

Clay said. "I'm here because it'll cost me money if I have to drive them across the Sink."

"You want me to cry about it?" Elkhart snapped.

For a moment Clay's temper almost slipped. Again he caught himself in time. He peered back through the cottonwoods. The Arrow hands were still watching him. He wondered where Lon Perry might be. He faced around again.

"We'd be obliged if you'd let us go through your fence, Elkhart."

Elkhart leaned forward, glaring down over the porch rail. "You boys are in for a rough summer," Elkhart said, "if I want to make it rough."

Clay felt a pressure at his temples. He glanced at the windows behind Elkhart and wondered if someone in there had a rifle trained on his breastbone. Cold sweat chilled the back of his neck, but he did not show his apprehension. His brown face was as tight as it had been when the Mexican army officers questioned him endlessly about the rifles he had hidden for delivery to Monjosa.

"Don't be a stiff-necked fool," he warned.

"Or your neighbors will ride with wire cutters in their saddlebags."

"I'll shoot the man that cuts my fence."

Clay picked up his reins. "Now we know where we stand. I told the boys I might have a talk with you. And I have. I've done my part."

He thought he saw a touch of worry on the big man's face, but he couldn't be sure. What did Elkhart have to worry about? The man probably had twenty-five riders, a lot of credit at the bank and a sheriff who would do his bidding.

"Things might be different," Elkhart said, "if Nina was my wife and Joe Alford hadn't come sneaking back—"

"Maybe Nina Alford won't like this high-handed way of yours," Clay said. "After all, she's one of the basin ranchers." He saw Elkhart chewing this over, and added, "What'll it take for you to put a gate in that fence?"

"A fence keeps out trespassers," Elkhart snapped. "I been in this country a long time. I'm tired of neighbors crowding me."

"Then you won't do anything about a gate," Clay said quietly.

Elkhart seemed to be on edge. He kept

glancing at the men at the far end of the yard as if to make sure they were still handy.

"For Nina's sake I'll make a deal," Elkhart said. "Two bits a head for all the beef driven through my fence."

Clay gave a short laugh. "If you figure to charge me four hundred dollars for the herd I've got you'll have a long wait."

"You'll pay or you'll drive across the Sink," Elkhart said angrily.

Clay reined his horse away from the porch. "We'll see about that," he told the rancher.

Just as he started across the yard Lon Perry and five men rode through an opening between the corral and some sheds. At sight of Clay the gunman drew rein.

When Perry made a move toward his gun, Elkhart cried, "Let him ride out, Lon!"

"But don't he know about—" Perry broke off.

"Know about what?" Clay said.

Elkhart had come down the steps to stand half a dozen yards behind Clay. "You better get out, Janner," he advised. "Now!"

Clay looked at Perry's tight face, the small cold eyes. The men with him were all cut from the same pattern, and all loaded for bear.

Without a word he put spurs to his horse. Many questions needed answering, but this wasn't the time. Not with those odds against him. He rode at a gallop the length of the yard, past the men with the rifles. The young, bald man shouted an obscenity and Clay was tempted to pull up and do something about it. But he couldn't. Those tough-hands in the yard would like nothing better than to end it. They'd have done it already if Elkhart hadn't checked them.

Why had Elkhart done that?

As he rode on, he realized that he did know the answer to that one. Nina Alford had not yet made up her mind, and that had prevented Elkhart from giving the order to jump him. It was a sorry situation, he thought as he cut along the valley floor, when a woman could call the turn between war and peace simply by deciding whether to go back to her husband or marry another man.

At the eastern rim of the valley Clay ran into a fence crew stringing wire. Coils of the stuff were still piled high on a flatbed wagon. The crew eyed him sullenly. One of them picked up a rifle and put it down again. They let him ride through the small gap that remained open in this vicinity, but before many more days

Elkhart would have his entire range sealed off with that cussed stuff known as bobwire.

Five miles farther on Clay ran into Buck Bogarth who was driving to his ranch with a wagon-load of supplies. Bogarth pulled in the team and listened to Clay's account of his visit with Elkhart.

"Two bits a head," the rancher said in disgust. "Ain't a one of us can pay that kind of money."

"If Elkhart wants to get rich," Clay said, "he better watch out that he don't get rich and dead all at the same time."

Bogarth looked grim. "I like Joe Alford, but if he'd stayed in Mexico we'd be havin' a better time of it here. But we still got hope, maybe. If Nina marries Elkhart then we'll get that gate in the fence. And it won't cost no two bits a head. My wife had a talk with Nina. And that's what Nina said, in so many words."

"Friendship must not mean a damn to you," Clay said shortly. The sun seemed to be baking the back of his neck. He felt out of sorts from his talk with Elkhart, and here was another gutless rancher like Joe Alford. Or almost as bad. Letting his whole future ride on a woman's whim.

96

Bogarth glared at him. "Joe's my friend, all right," he said heatedly. "But I stand to lose everything—"

"Unless Joe's wife marries Elkhart," Clay finished for him and gave a grunt of disgust. "Don't count on Nina turning down her husband. I've got a hunch they'll make up yet."

"You think so?" Bogarth snapped. "I just left Joe at Fierro's. He's on a drunk. Him and Nina had another fight. And I reckon this was the last one."

Bogarth whipped up his team and drove off. Clay sat his saddle a moment, staring at the distant peaks of the Sabers. Up there, the pass which led directly to the railroad had been blocked off by Elkhart's fence. And on top of all his other troubles Joe had to go and get on a drunk.

Angrily Clay turned his horse toward Reeder Wells. Married life, he thought. If there's any good part of it, I've never seen it yet.

Why didn't he just take off and to hell with Joe? Yet he felt a certain loyalty. There was something likable about Joe Alford, despite his faults. And he had known Joe a long time. Since they'd punched cows together years back in west Texas.

It was nearly dark by the time Clay came out on the trail above Reeder Wells and saw the glowing lights of the dismal little town far below. As he rode down the steep grade he could feel the hot evening breeze blowing off the Sink to the west. A man forced to drive his herd across the Sink would cut its value by at least twenty-five percent, he had learned.

Well, Elkhart was putting on the squeeze, but good. He'd end up owning the whole valley and do it without firing a gun. Do it with his forty-mile fence.

In a black mood Clay rode up to Fierro's and dismounted in front of the squat 'dobe saloon. There were few people on the walks. He entered the cantina and Fierro, looking fierce with his spiked mustaches, nodded his black head at Joe Alford. Alford was slumped at the corner table where the basin ranchers had held their pow-wow not too long ago.

"Crudo," Fierro said. "Drunk and sick. I try to get him to stop drinking, but—" The Mexican spread his dark hands and hoisted his shoulders ear-high.

Clay walked over and got Alford by the hair and jerked his head up from the table. Alford blinked at him out of bloodshot eyes that could not quite focus. His mouth hung open.

"I'll have to tie him to a saddle," Clay said.

"But he does not wish to go home," Fierro said in Spanish.

"He's going home," Clay said, "and he's going to like it. So is his wife going to like it. I'm getting damned sick of this."

He gave a boy two bits and told him to go to the livery and get Alford's horse and bring it to the cantina. Then he went to a cafe across the street, got a pot of black coffee and forced Alford to drink it. Alford spilled most of the first cup down the front of his shirt. The scalding helped to revive him.

The three customers at the bar watched all this with faint interest. Fierro stood by, wiping his hands on a greasy apron, shaking his head from side to side.

"It is bad when a man has trouble with his wife," Fierro said. "He then does not have the sense of a goat."

A sudden silence in the bar made Clay look up. He was holding the pot of coffee in one hand, steadying Joe Alford on his chair with the other. A tall fleshless man with a star on his shirt had entered the cantina. He let the swing doors flap shut and came tramping across the dirt floor. Clay noticed a wavering uncertainty in his brown eyes.

This, then, was Sheriff Bert Lynden—and no wonder Byrd Elkhart had found him so easy to buy. Not a forceful man, this sheriff. Backed by the power of his badge and the prestige of Elkhart's Arrow Ranch, he still seemed unsure of himself.

"You're Janner," Lynden said, and Clay nodded. The men at the bar were all attention now. Fierro had quietly faded away from Alford's table, leaving the three of them alone.

Alford goggled dazedly at Lynden. "What's the matter, Sheriff?" he said thickly.

"I came down here to nip a range war in the bud," the sheriff said. He went into detail, telling how he had arrived last night from the county seat.

"If there's any range war, it's Elkhart's doing," Clay said.

The sheriff lowered his gaze, seemed to be trying to marshal his thoughts. At last he looked up, hooking his thumbs in the wide shell belt which he wore under an old gray coat.

"Now about them six cows," he said. "Elkhart was fully justified in—"

Clay set down the coffee pot. He stepped away from the table. "What six cows?" he said.

The sheriff blinked. "Why, the six that busted through Elkhart's fence. Them Chihuahuas you and Alford brought back from Mexico."

"None of our cows were anywhere near that fence," Clay said.

The sheriff looked more uncertain than ever. "But I hear you went over to Elkhart's today."

"To talk to him about putting a gate in that fence," Clay said. "You haven't told me yet about those six cows. You better start talking, Sheriff."

Bert Lynden backed up a step and put a hand on his gun. "This is the law you're talkin' to," he said with a shrill dignity. "I won't take your lip."

The men at the bar had crowded up close, expecting trouble. They looked from the sheriff with his pale, fleshless face, to the tall Texan known as Clay Janner.

"Them six cows busted through Elkhart's fence," the sheriff said. "Some of his men shot 'em."

Clay felt the blood drain from his face. "He had six head of beef killed?"

"They busted his fence," the sheriff said defensively.

"The dirty sonofabitch."

Lynden took another backward step. "Now don't you go talkin' like that. We got a jail here. I'll lock you up, Janner. Sure as hell, I'll lock you up."

Alford had got shakily to his feet. For the first time he seemed to realize what was going on. "Elkhart had no right to do that, Sheriff."

"He had every right. Elkhart is sorry his men took it into their own hands, but after all—" Lynden stood tensely, gripping his holstered gun.

Clay forced himself to take a deep breath to quiet his jumping nerves. "Whereabouts did this happen, Sheriff?"

"Squaw Creek," the sheriff said, and cleared his throat twice. "What I come here to tell you is this. I don't want no trouble from you, Janner. Elkhart's sorry it happened, but like I say he was within his rights. So you just tuck your tail and figure you're lucky there wasn't more of your cows busted that fence."

"Who brought the word to you, Sheriff?" Clay made himself drawl. "About me being at Elkhart's today?"

102

"Why, Baldy Renson."

Clay remembered the bald young man he had seen that afternoon at Elkhart's. And it meant that Elkhart had sent Baldy Renson high-tailing it for town to give the story to the sheriff.

"No wonder Elkhart was edgy today," Clay said. "He figured I'd come out to Arrow to raise hell about those dead cows. And I didn't even know about it." He gave the sheriff a tight grin. "Looks like the joke's on me, Sheriff."

Lynden squinted at him suspiciously. "Just so you take it this way there'll be no trouble. Just don't go and try to settle with Elkhart for this business."

"Elkhart must've yelled mighty loud to get you down from the county seat, eh, Sheriff?" Clay said, still in that drawling voice.

"He did—" The sheriff broke off. "I had some business down here anyhow. I do no man's bidding."

Someone in the cantina laughed softly. The sheriff wheeled to see who had laughed. But everyone wore a straight face. At last Lynden faced around to Clay again.

"Just so we understand each other. Them six cows is dead. They busted a fence. There's nothing you can do about it. Understand?"

103

"Sure, I understand."

The sheriff frowned painfully, trying to read something in Clay's mild manner. "Don't you try nothing or you'll be in my jail." With that he wheeled and clumped out of the cantina.

The tension in the place eased off. The drinkers went back to the bar to talk over this latest development. Clay put a hand on Alford's shoulder.

"You get for home, Joe," he said in a low voice. "I'm staying in town tonight. Got some business."

Alford wavered up on his feet, both hands resting on the table top to support his shaky weight. "Listen, Clay, don't go after Elkhart—"

Clay shook his head. "I've just got an idea I might scare up a cattle buyer. Get somebody to buy our herd and contract to drive it to the railroad. They'll have all the grief, not us. Then we'll be out from under."

Alford studied Clay's face out of his blood-shot eyes. "You're lyin' to me, Clay."

"If I'm lucky we can take our money and clear out. Montana, maybe. Providing you haven't made up with Nina."

"I don't want to leave her, Clay," Alford said miserably.

"Good. Then get for home and act like a husband. Not like a whipped dog."

Clay finally got him outside and into the saddle of the horse the boy had brought down from the stable. When Alford was headed in the direction of Spade, Clay went back into the cantina. He had a drink of Mexican brandy with Fierro.

Making sure no one was close enough to eavesdrop, he asked, "Just how does a fella go about getting to Squaw Creek?"

Fierro's black eyes glinted appreciatively. "You are one damn fool, senor. But I would do the same if I wore your boots. Squaw Creek is fifteen miles south—"

8

THAT night Clay stayed in the one-story New Mexico Hotel. He got up at daybreak and had a breakfast of leathery hotcakes in the cafe. He rode out of town, ostensibly heading for Spade, but when he reached the ridge he swung southwest, following the landmarks Fierro had given him last night. Maybe he was a fool to trust the Mexican. But he sensed the man was not on Elkhart's side of the fence, and in a business such as this you had to trust somebody.

With the morning sun warming him, he felt almost light-hearted. That is, he could have felt that way except for the constant pressures riding him. He wanted to relax, let the horse pick its own trail. He saw a flash of color ahead as a bluejay dipped out of the junipers. In the distance, fleecy white clouds lay low on the horizon. In that direction lay Mexico. Despite the months of imprisonment he had suffered there, the land held something for him. He liked the people. Not the insufferable Federal officers who rode roughshod over the peons, but the people themselves. Maybe he'd go there instead of Montana. No icy winds of the north to cut a man like the lash of a whip. Just warm skies and . . .

He felt a tightening of his nerves. He pulled in the roan horse, glanced back toward Reeder Wells. Nothing moved in the junipers. The sun sent a shaft of golden light along the canyon he had just left.

Even though he could see nothing he felt that he was being followed. And his horse sensed it. The animal was restless, taut.

Well, did I expect anything less? he asked himself.

He continued on, slower now. At a promontory he moved into a thicket, dismounted and crept back with his rifle. For a long time he lay there watching the trail below, without catching sign of anyone. Whoever was back there was an expert in this sort of business. He had anticipated Clay's move and holed up.

Clay started on again, almost convinced that his senses had played tricks on him. He was too keyed up, he tried to tell himself. But even though he argued against it he knew someone was back there.

For a mile he kept the roan at a steady lope, then drew rein and listened. No sound. Nothing but the wind blowing hot off the Sink.

At last he came to Squaw Creek. Because of the dry months only a trickle of muddy water moved crookedly along the sand. Even without the creek for a landmark he would have known the spot. Twenty yards from the creek a great gap had been torn in the barbed wire fence. Some of the posts had been uprooted. A black cloud of buzzards rose from the remains of the slaughtered Chihuahua steers. The six steers, already bloated, lay well inside the fence.

The buzzards flapped their wings and ran, many of them so gorged that they could hardly rise from the ground.

He had wanted to see this for himself, and now he had. Elkhart had deliberately done this deed to provoke a war. He started to swing down, and noticed the twitching of the roan's ears. He reined the horse aside just as a piece of lead whined viciously past his face. Then came the sharp report of a rifle.

Digging in the spurs, Clay sent the roan plunging into the underbrush. He flung himself from the saddle, rifle in hand. He struck the ground hard, rolled, as another shot came whistling from a stand of aspens higher up the slope.

He lay quite still on the ground, head turned so he could watch the slope. He had lost his hat when he quit the saddle. The roan had kept on for a few yards, then veered off into some scraggly cottonwoods along the creek bank. It halted and began to graze on the sparse brown grass.

The rifle fire had sent the buzzards on another wing-beating retreat. Now in the renewed quiet they came floating back to the six dead steers like a black cloud.

Still Clay remained motionless. The sun rose higher. In a few more minutes it would be in his eyes, blinding him to the movements of the ambusher above. Already the sun was touching the rocks just above Clay's head.

His mouth was dry. He cursed himself for being careless. But the sight of the dead steers had sent such a surge of rage through him that he had forgotten the danger behind him.

In another minute he would have to move. He couldn't afford to have the sun in his eyes. And that would be a cue for the ambusher to send down another bullet. At first Clay could not understand why the man didn't try and finish the job. Then he realized only his body from the waist down would be in view of the man above. The rocks cut off the rest of it.

Just when Clay was about to shift his body, he heard someone coming cautiously down the hill. Desperately he tried to catch a glimpse of the man, knowing that in his haste to play dead he had misjudged the skulker's position. The man was a dozen yards to Clay's left instead of directly above as he had assumed.

The footsteps halted. A man said, "Hey, down there."

Clay did not recognize the voice. It wasn't Lon Perry or Elkhart; that much he was sure of.

The man said, "Move out where I can get a look at you." Then, when Clay didn't answer, he tried again. "You shot bad? I got some whisky here."

Clay didn't stir. He could hear the roan chomping grass. The buzzards were fluttering beyond the broken fence as if torn between potential danger and the lure of the feast on the ground.

"I can see your legs," the man above said. "I'll put a bullet through 'em if you don't answer up."

Sweat dripped from Clay's forehead, stung his eyes. Bit by bit it soaked his shirt and plastered the cloth to his body. The sun rose higher.

Suddenly Clay jerked back his legs, rolled himself into a tight knot. A rifle bullet plowed into the ground where his feet had been, throwing sand in his face. Momentarily blinded, he flung himself back, landing hard on his left shoulder. He let go of his rifle, dug for his short gun.

Now he could see the man plainly, only a few feet up the slope. It was Baldy, the man he had seen yesterday afternoon at Elkhart's Arrow. Surprise showed on Baldy's face as he tried to bring his rifle to bear on the shifting target below. Clay fired from a prone position on the ground. Baldy leaped aside, scared now. He tried to center the rifle, but before he could squeeze off a shot, a bullet from Clay's gun crashed into his chest. Arms loose, the bald man fell headfirst down the slope. He rolled a few feet, and then the rocks caught him.

The buzzards were flapping their wings again. The roan had looked up from its graze. Clay advanced, sweating, his revolver cocked. He picked up the man's rifle and threw it into the brush. Then with one hand he caught the man by an arm, dragged him the rest of the way down the slope.

Baldy Renson sat with his back to the rocks, holding his arms across his chest. Already blood had soaked the front of his shirt and was beginning to stain the sleeves.

Clay drew Baldy's revolver and threw it after the rifle.

"You're new at this business," he said.

Renson just looked at him. Pallor was spreading across his face.

"Why didn't Elkhart send Lon Perry? He's the expert in this sort of thing, isn't he?"

"Go to hell," Renson said through his teeth.

Clay shrugged. "Is there a doctor in Reeder Wells?"

"Yeah."

"I can leave you out here to die alone," Clay said, "or I can take you to town. It's up to you."

"Die?" Renson said. "I ain't shot that bad— am I?" He looked down at the red ruin of his shirt and his jaw wobbled loosely as he opened his mouth and shut it and opened it again. "Listen, I didn't want to get mixed up in this.

But Elkhart give me two hundred dollars. He—"

"Why you? Why not Lon Perry?"

"Kee-ryst get me to town, Janner."

Clay searched the man to make sure there was no hideout under the stained shirt. Then with a bandanna he tried to plug the chest wound. He tied the bandanna in place with strips torn from Renson's shirt.

He got his roan and rode after Renson's horse tied in the aspens above. When he boosted Renson into the saddle, Renson made a half-hearted attempt to steal his gun. Clay slapped his hand away and stepped back.

"I hope you live long enough to get to town," Clay said. "I want the sheriff to hear how his good friend Elkhart paid you to try and murder me."

"Maybe I won't talk." Renson's voice was feeble now. He was holding to the saddle-horn with both hands.

"I ought to leave you out here to die," Clay said. "It's probably what you'd have done to me. Or maybe been merciful and put a bullet between my eyes." He snorted scornfully. "You'll need me, friend. You'll need me bad. Before the hour's gone you won't be able to set

113

that saddle alone. I'll have to tie you. I'll have to lead your horse to town. Now do you want to go it alone or do you want me to help?"

"Just get me to the doc's." Baldy took one hand from the saddle-horn and pressed it against his bandaged chest. "I guess you're a whiter man than Elkhart claims. Else you'd finish me."

"So Elkhart thinks I'm bad, huh?"

Renson nodded.

They started back over the trail from town. Clay kept looking beyond the broken fence, looking for sign of Elkhart's men, but he saw nothing.

"Elkhart says you got a gun rep," Renson said thickly. "You marshaled down at Paso Del Norte. Cleaned it up, he says."

"You were a fool to take his money and try this."

"He said you'd get steamed up when you come out and seen them dead cows. I was to wait till you got on Arrow property and then shoot you. But I couldn't wait. I figured to drag you over afterwards—"

"Then what?"

"Elkhart said I was supposed to tell my story to the sheriff. How you come out to look over

114

them dead cows and tried to kill me where I was left guardin' the break in the fence. After I told my story I was to head outa this country and never come back."

"You work cheap," Clay said. "My God, two hundred dollars to kill a man!"

Renson bent lower in the saddle. "He wouldn't come after you himself. Or send Perry because—" His voice trailed away.

Clay pulled up, steadying the man. "Because after you'd pulled out of the country he could claim it wasn't his idea to kill me. He could say you acted on your own. You'd be long gone and in no position to tell the truth even if you wanted to."

"He done it on account of that Alford woman," Renson said hoarsely. "He wants his skirts clean on account of her. And he don't want her to turn against Lon Perry. He figures he's got to use Perry in these parts for a long time—"

Baldy swayed again. Clay got a saddle rope and started to tie him. But Renson told him in a shaky voice that he'd have to rest. Clay helped him out of the saddle and to the shade of a cut bank.

There was a wild light in Renson's eyes now

and Clay knew fever had gripped him. Renson began to laugh. "Elkhart sure was sore at Perry for cuttin' the fence and makin' out like your cows busted it. And then shootin' them cows. When you rode out to Arrow yesterday Elkhart figured you'd come to do some shootin'—"

Renson keeled over on his side. Clay felt for his pulse. There was none.

"Lucky to last this long," Clay said aloud, and wondered what to do next.

If he took the body to town, the sheriff would have an excuse to lock him up. They could even hang him for Renson's murder, providing Elkhart had as great a hold on the politics of the county as everybody seemed to believe.

It was a chill prospect any way you looked at it. At last he made his decision. He dragged Renson's body back into the brush and covered it with rocks. Then he led Renson's horse high up on the rim and turned it loose. The animal headed in the direction of Arrow.

He knew that Elkhart would find the riderless horse and draw his own conclusions. Maybe he'd send the sheriff after one Clay Janner. Maybe he'd play his cards close to the vest and figure another plan.

It was full dark before Clay reached Spade.

He stumbled over something in the yard. It was Joe Alford. At first he thought Alford had been shot. Then, striking a match, he saw the empty bottle at Alford's side.

No lights showed in the house, but the bunkhouse was lighted. Sam Lennox, having heard someone ride in, came to the yard. "Figured maybe it was you, boss," the black-bearded rider said. "Hell's busted loose since you been gone. We just got word that six of them Chihuahuas got killed when they're supposed to have busted Elkhart's fence. Which is a damn lie, if you ask me."

"I know all about it," Clay said. "Help me get Alford on his feet."

"Where you figure on takin' him?" Lennox asked after they heaved the big man erect.

"To the house. Where he belongs."

"I dunno whether the missus will let him stay or not. They argued most of the day and—"

"I can handle him now, Sam. Thanks."

Clay walked Alford across the yard and up the porch steps. Nina must have heard them, for she opened the front door. She carried a lamp. When she saw Clay, she stiffened, then looked angrily at her drunken husband. She clutched a green wrapper across her night dress.

Her long blonde hair hung down her back in two braids.

"I don't want him here," she said thinly. "Not until he sobers up."

Clay made no reply. He walked Alford into the bedroom and dumped him on the bed. He pulled off Alford's boots and threw them in a corner of the room.

Finally Nina picked up a blanket and put it over her snoring husband. "He's so helpless," she said.

"If you didn't fight with him all the time," Clay said, "he wouldn't be drunk like this."

Her gray eyes flared, but then the fire seemed to go out of them. "After fourteen months Joe thinks he has some rights as a husband."

"It's about time you made up your mind," Clay told her bluntly. "Either kick Joe out or take him back. If you don't, this country will blow up in your face."

"You can't blame conditions on me, Clay Janner."

"Elkhart's been playing it easy so far on account of you," Clay said. "But if you don't quit leading him on—" He made a cutting motion with his hand. "Oh, to hell with it!"

As he started out of the room she touched his

arm with the tips of her fingers. "I suppose you and Joe had a grand time in Mexico. Getting drunk, things like that."

He looked her up and down. "You're not much of a wife," he said coldly.

"You're insulting," she said, but there was a lack of venom in her voice. He could see her breasts stirring under the wrapper as she drew a deep breath.

"You're a funny woman, all right," he said. "You don't worry about your neighbors or whether Elkhart will freeze them out. All you worry about is whether your husband had a good time while he was away from you."

"It's important to me," she said.

He studied her. She was a looker, he had to admit. He couldn't blame Joe Alford for bragging about her during those long days in prison.

"Yeah, we had fun in Mexico," he said. "We had a room smaller than this bedroom. There was usually water on the floor. We had some fine friends—rats. Sometimes they'd bite if we didn't fight them off. There was always a battle between us to see who got the food."

She followed him to the parlor, her high heels rapping on the floor. He caught her scent and his nerves tingled.

"It's a very fine story," she said, "but somehow I don't believe it."

"Joe has more faith in you than you have in him."

"I suppose you mean about Elkhart and me?" She swallowed. "That's where you're wrong. Joe stood in this room and accused me—"

"He doesn't really think that," Clay said. "Joe's been hurt, that's all. He'll get over it."

"Don't you think I've been hurt? Or isn't that important to a man? A woman can sit and wait and do nothing to cause the slightest bit of gossip. But a man—" Her whole body quivered with indignation. "Where were you last night and today? Sampling the pleasures of Reeder Wells?"

"You'd be surprised what I've been doing," he said heavily, and thought of Baldy Renson. He walked out.

Because he didn't want to answer questions, he got his blanket from the bunkhouse and went to the cottonwoods near the barn. The crowded bunkhouse would be depressing tonight. The men would want to know where he'd been and he hadn't made up his mind yet whether to take even Sam Lennox into his confidence concerning the death of Renson.

Besides, since his imprisonment in Mexico, he liked sleeping out under the stars. Here a man could think straight and forget the prison. Far back in the cottonwoods he rolled a cigarette and lit it. Dark forebodings plagued him.

9

SHORTLY after supper Byrd Elkhart shut himself up in his office. He was in a black mood and he seemed unable to shake it off. Every time he thought of Nina and Joe together under the same roof he wanted to take a gun and finish it. But he knew this wasn't the way. This afternoon he had met Russ Hagen at the fence and the man had dutifully reported that Alford was not getting along with his wife at all. They quarreled a great deal, Hagen had said, and Alford had finally gone on a drunk. This might be true, Elkhart had told Hagen, but still, fighting or not, Joe Alford was sharing a house with Nina.

Hagen rubbed a hand over the knot behind his right ear. "I'm just waitin' for a chance to tangle with Janner," he said. "The son hit me when I wasn't lookin'."

"Well, next time look!"

"Don't worry. I'm goin' to fix his face so his own mother would think it was somethin' somebody dug out from under a rock."

"Maybe you won't have to tangle with Janner after all," Elkhart said. He was thinking of the assignment he had given Baldy Renson. But he must have had a premonition, for he added, "Just in case Clay Janner has a streak of luck, finish him next time."

"Don't worry."

"With your fists. Not a gun. Understand?"

Hagen had ridden back to Spade and Elkhart returned to Arrow. Several times during the day Elkhart had an urge to ride to town and see the excitement—and view Janner's body in the shed behind the New Mexico Hotel which served as the morgue of Reeder Wells. But he held himself in. To keep his mind off Janner that day he kept himself busy. He helped break a horse, something he had not done in years. It kept his mind off Nina, too.

When he left the breaking pen, sweating, dead tired, Lon Perry fell in step with him. "Sure hell to be in love with a married woman, ain't it, Byrd?"

Elkhart stiffened. He resented Perry's familiarity, but decided to overlook it. Right now he needed Perry's gun. But if the time ever came when he had to face up to Perry, he felt up to the job.

"I've been in love with Nina for a long time," Elkhart said, and paused to take a dipper of water from a bucket on the house porch. "A damn long time before that no-good Alford showed up."

Elkhart drank the cool water, hung the dipper back on the edge of the barrel. Joe Alford's return had been unsettling enough, but Alford's partner was even more of a threat. Elkhart had sized Clay Janner up at their first meeting and judged him to be no man to fool with. Janner was the one stirring up the basin ranchers. He had to be. He was the one with the guts.

As he told the judge one night over a bottle: "This fence of mine will show the boys their day is done around here. It's not forty miles of fence like I claim, but it sounds good. Anyhow, I've got enough wire to fence them off from the pass. That's all that counts. When they see I mean business they'll sell out. Or they'll pay a toll."

"Or drive across the Sink," the judge put in. He was a small, watery-eyed man. He poured two drinks to Elkhart's one. "You can't get away with it, Byrd."

"I can and will," Elkhart retorted. He edged

forward in his chair. "I've got a contract with Triple X in Chicago. It's the biggest contract a packing house ever gave a ranch in this territory." His voice was shaking with excitement. "That means I've got to have more graze. Those fools in the basin are licked already. If they sell out they'll have a few dollars to get a start somewheres else—"

"But if it goes to court," the judge warned, "you won't win."

Elkhart watched him pour another drink. "You better play your cards right, Judge," Elkhart said coldly. "If you do you might be a senator. But you'd need my backing to swing it."

The judge frowned thoughtfully and seemed to relish the idea. He tossed off his drink. "Just don't let it get to court, Byrd."

"Don't worry. It won't."

"These things are better done in the dark of the moon," the judge said in parting.

And then, just as Elkhart got set to put on the pressure, Joe Alford had returned home—with this tough-hand Janner to side him.

Now, in his small office, Byrd Elkhart eyed a bottle on his desk. He extended a hand for it, then shook his head. No, he wouldn't let liquor weaken him. It had ruined too many men in this country.

He was about to blow out the lamp when he heard a commotion in the yard. Buckling on his gunbelt, he went outside. Some of the men had gathered around a horse. One of them held a lantern.

Lon Perry saw Elkhart coming from the house and moved to intercept him. "Renson's horse," Lon Perry said, jerking a thumb over his shoulder.

"Where's Renson?"

"Just the horse. Not Renson," Perry said significantly. Elkhart drew a deep breath and let it out slowly. "I see," he said. "Blood on the saddle?"

"No. The reins were tied to the saddle-horn."

"I'll be damned," Elkhart said, clenching his big hands. The man with the lantern was leading the horse toward the corral.

"We could take the boys and ride to Spade and get Mr. Janner outa bed. We could rope him to a good tree."

Elkhart gave a quick shake of his head. "I want to stay out of it."

"Then I'll go."

"We'll wait and see what develops."

"You should've let me go after Janner," Lon Perry said bitterly. "Now you wasted two hundred dollars. Janner's got it and he's laughing at you."

"We're going to be around these parts for a long time, Lon," the rancher said. "So we're going to move cautiously."

"And while you move cautiously," Perry sneered, "you'll lose your fence—and lose the girl."

"Keep Nina's name out of this," Elkhart said. "We'd be in good shape now if you hadn't got that bright idea to drive some of Janner's cows to the fence and shoot them."

"It'll still be a good idea," Perry said, and smiled in the darkness. "We'll have Clay Janner swinging from the end of a rope. You'll see."

He started away but Elkhart caught him by an elbow, swinging him around. "We'll ride up to Squaw Creek tomorrow and see if we can back-track Baldy's horse. If we can locate his body we'll take it to the sheriff. That's all we'll need to bring Janner to the rope. But we'll do it my way. Understand?"

"So you're goin' to ease up on Alford, huh?"

"We'll keep the pressure on him. If he keeps

on drinking like Russ Hagen says he is, he'll do some damn fool thing that'll get his head blown off."

"Wouldn't be surprised," Lon Perry said.

Elkhart went back to the house and tried to sleep. But all he could think of was Nina Alford and her drunken no-good husband.

10

IN the quiet of the dark cottonwoods beyond
the barn, Clay Janner tried to bring the
objectives of his life into focus. He stared
up through the leafy branches at the stars
blinking in the clear New Mexican sky. What
would he do next, providing he managed to sell
the herd of Chihuahuas? Drift on to some new
territory, meet new women, make money, lose
it. Never with any roots. Always planning to
settle down in some locality, but at the last
moment pulling up stakes to move somewhere
else. He wondered where he would be today
if he had stayed put as Elkhart had. There
were many things he didn't like about the
man, but Elkhart had become a success and
that seemed to be all that counted. He had a
sheriff and, according to the pool ranchers, a
judge.

Hell, Elkhart had the power of life and death
over his neighbors. Or it amounted to that.
They failed or succeeded only if Elkhart allowed
them room in which to grow. But still the town

of Reeder Wells seemed to respect him. Fear him, anyway.

Powerful as he was, Elkhart could hire a novice like Baldy Renson and set him against an experienced man like Clay Janner. The odds might be all against Renson, but that didn't matter. Lying here in the darkness, Clay couldn't help but feel sorry for the man. Renson had played the game smart enough while he was trailing his quarry. But once it came to the handling of guns he had no chance.

A sound in the darkness beyond the trees caused him to snatch his gun from under his blanket and sit up. Someone was coming toward him. Just as he was about to order a halt, he saw a woman's figure outlined in the moonlight. It was Nina Alford. She spoke his name. She came up to him and stood looking down at him. She had put on a shirtwaist and skirt. Drawing the skirt about her ankles, she sank down to the ground.

He put away his gun, feeling embarrassed somehow. "How'd you know I was out here?" he demanded.

"I saw you strike a match when you lit your cigarette." She sat so near that he caught her scent and it stirred him. "Joe's still passed out," she said and ran the tip of her tongue over her lips. "He won't wake up until noon, probably. He never does when he's like this."

The statement sent his nerves to humming, but he did not let on that her bold declaration affected him. "You better get back to the house." He threw away his cigarette. It lay glowing at the base of a tree. "What if one of the men saw you come out here?"

"Why should you care? You think little enough of me as it is."

"I like Joe."

"And maybe I like him," she whispered. She arched her body, resting her weight on her hands, and peered up at the moon. "How were the girls in Mexico?" she asked suddenly. "The ones you and Joe had."

"I told you once," he said. "There were no girls. Besides, that's a hell of a thing for a married woman to ask a man."

"Don't lie to me, please. Joe had a girl, didn't he?"

"What do you want me to do? Swear on my mother's grave?"

He could see moonlight reflected in her eyes. "You mean to tell me that for fourteen months Joe didn't have a woman?" She gave a scornful laugh and nudged his arm with her elbow. "Tell me the truth."

She was so close he could feel her warm breath against his cheek. "It's not smart to push a man like this."

"Just tell me the truth about Joe."

He clamped a hand on her arm as one of the horses nickered in the corral, but there was no further sound. She relaxed and he dropped his hand from her arm. She moved against him then and he was aware of her softness.

Suddenly he caught her by the shoulders and found her mouth. She came alive, clinging to him. Then, after a moment, she pushed him away. She sat looking at him. Then she began to weep and laugh all at the same time. The sounds were awesome there in the darkness.

Puzzled by her behavior, he got up. She rose unsteadily to her feet.

"This is what I really wanted to find out," she said hoarsely. "This great friendship. Yours and Joe's. You're a gun runner, a cheap saddle bum who profits from the misery of others."

"Hold on with that kind of talk," he warned.

"A man who puts guns in the hands of peons when they need bread."

"How else do you think they'll get bread

132

except with a gun? They're sick of Diaz down there. They'll follow Monjosa until somebody else better comes along. And I admire their guts."

"But I hardly admire yours," she said scornfully. "Trying to make love to your best friend's wife."

He leaned close. "I had a low opinion of you when Joe and I came home and found you alone with Elkhart. Don't make it any lower with this sort of crazy business."

She stepped back, defiantly hooking her left hand at the V of her shirtwaist. "What if I tear my clothes? And scream?"

"Go ahead."

"Joe would come," she said, "and you know what he'd try and do."

"So that's your idea," Clay said. "Coming out here and—"

"You'll have to get on your horse and ride. Because Joe is your friend and you won't want to take a gun to him. If you stay Joe will try and kill you—" Suddenly she bent her head and began to weep again. But this time there was no hysteria. This time the sobs were low, choked.

"Half of that herd is mine," he told her. "I paid for it with my blood. I'm not going to ride off and leave it. No matter what you figure to tell Joe about this."

"Why can't Joe be like you? Why can't he talk up to people? Talk up to me?"

He couldn't stand it any longer. "Maybe you planned for me to kill Joe," he snarled. "Then you could marry Elkhart—"

She slapped him hard across the face. She hooked her fingers to use her nails on him. He caught her wrists with one hand and jerked her against him. Her face came against his and the life seemed to go out of her. She sagged and her lips moved across his cheek and to his mouth.

"Oh, Clay—"

Her abrupt change of mood frightened him. He held her off, knowing he could not fight her for long. She was soft and warm and the prison dungeon at San Sebastian had starved him, left him woman hungry. She was Joe Alford's wife, he told himself. And she was no good. She and Elkhart together while her husband rotted in a Mexican prison. . . .

"Get back to the house," he said.

She seemed utterly spent. "Please believe me, Clay. I didn't want you to kill Joe. Not so I could marry Elkhart." She stepped toward him, her eyes swollen from her weeping. "Maybe I

134

did have a crazy idea about making you leave. Before you brought real trouble to us. But—"

"You can still scream," he reminded her.

"That was a nasty threat to make. I'm sorry." She peered at his tall figure in the shadows of the cottonwoods. "That story about you and Joe in prison. Was it really the truth?"

"Yeah. I wish to hell it wasn't."

Her shoulders sagged. He put a hand on her arm, feeling the warm flesh beneath the thin material of her blouse. "Go home now, before Joe wakes up and misses you."

"Why couldn't I have married someone like you, Clay?"

"You married Joe instead."

"But why can't he be strong? Just once?" She moved away, then turned and looked back at him. Moonlight touched her pale hair. "I could love you, Clay. I could love you a lot. If I let myself."

She ran toward the house. He lay down in his blankets again. But sleep was a long time in coming.

Next day, Joe Alford seemed cheerful. He didn't even show signs of a hangover. "Nina poured black coffee into me last night," he explained when Clay found him outside the bunkhouse, washing up for breakfast. He nudged Clay. "Me and Nina made up. What do you think of that?"

"You're a lucky man," Clay said glumly, wondering how long it would last.

"Nina likes you, Clay. She says you're a good friend. A real friend."

Clay thoughtfully ran a thumb along the brown line of his jaw. "It only proves there's no figuring women," he mumbled, and let it go at that. At least one thing was settled, temporarily.

For the next several days they worked roundup, and after Clay and his men had helped with the Spade herd, he rode with Alford to Reeder Wells. Leo Reese had sent one of his riders over to Spade with a message: it was time to ship beef. It was time to quit beating around the bush and reach a definite decision regarding Elkhart's fence.

Clay had seen these pools before. A group of frantic ranchers with more talk than guts, trying to buck one of the big outfits that held all the cards. He didn't see where a meeting would do much good but he agreed to accompany Alford. In addition to the .45 at his hip he wore a revolver under his shirt. There was no telling what sort of reception he might get from the sheriff. It was his first visit to town since the shooting of Baldy Renson. He had told no one of the incident, believing the fewer who knew about it the better. He had half-expected the sheriff to show up at the roundup camp with a posse and put him under arrest. But apparently Renson's body had not been found—And if it had been, Elkhart likely planned to do nothing about it. For the time being at least.

It was very hot when they rode into Reeder Wells. Dust curled up from the hoofs of their horses. A few dogs barked half-heartedly, then sought the shade of 'dobe walls. The moment they entered Fierro's, Clay felt the tension. He scanned the sprinkling of customers at the bar and along the walls. He turned his head and saw Lon Perry at the far end of the bar. The Arrow foreman had placed his hat on the bar beside a bottle. Pomade plastered his pale hair tight to his skull.

Fierro stood woodenly behind his bar.

A little way down the bar, Buck Bogarth was alternately licking his lips and mopping his brow with a bandanna.

"You boys holding a wake?" Clay asked the basin rancher.

Before Bogarth could reply, Lon Perry said, "If there's goin' to be a wake it'll be for you."

Clay stared the length of the room, meeting the gunman's small bright eyes. Then he stepped up to the bar and signaled Fierro to set out a bottle. Alford came up beside him, looking sick.

"Clay, let's drift," Alford said hoarsely.

Fierro, setting out a bottle, said in a tight whisper, "Get out, senor, while you can. Perry wait here for you. He wants to make the trouble."

Alford put a trembling hand on Clay's arm. "He's right, Clay. No use askin' for it."

"You can't always run," Clay said. "Sometime in your life you'll have to make a fight of it."

The rebuke stung and Alford flushed deeply. Instantly Clay regretted saying it. He closed his eyes, remembering how this big redhead, barehanded, had kept a Mexican officer from impaling him with a saber. He slapped Alford on the arm. "We'll make out, Joe," he whispered, and tried to grin. But Alford still looked sick.

Clay had his drink. Leo Reese and Shanley were sitting at a table, trying to play two-handed stud. They reminded him of mourners waiting for a funeral. Clay shifted his gaze through the window and saw four men cross the street and range themselves on the walk in front of the cantina. Two of them he recognized as having been with Perry the day of the stampede. Obviously the other two then were also Arrow men.

He felt a cold finger move slowly down his spine. This was a trap. He and the other pool members were boxed in this tight little building. The Elkhart men had drifted up nonchalantly the moment he and Alford had entered Fierro's. Well, he thought, a man can have only so much luck. You can outshoot fools like Baldy Renson, but somewhere along the line you're going to make a wrong move and walk right into it. This was Elkhart's town and Elkhart's sheriff. Elkhart's money and pressure could produce a dozen witnesses to satisfy a court that the events about to take place had been started by the pool. Sure. Eliminate competition in one grand move.

Leo Reese dropped a poker chip on the floor and the faint sound jarred his nerves. A wrong move or word would end in a lot of shooting and a lot of dying.

Lon Perry said, "A good friend of mine turned up missing, Janner. Maybe you know him. Baldy Renson."

Clay shrugged. "So?"

"His horse come back the other night. Baldy ain't come back yet. What about it?"

"I don't even know him," Clay answered. With a steady hand he poured a drink. He lifted the glass to his lips and downed it, never taking his eyes off Perry.

Perry, seeing that he was making no progress trying to rile Clay, turned his venom on Joe Alford. He gave the big nervous redhead a knowing smile. "Too bad you didn't stay in Mexico, Alford. By this time your wife and my boss would be married."

Men shifted their feet and moved away from Alford. "You're wrong, Perry," Alford said, choosing his words carefully. "As long as there was any chance of me bein' alive she wouldn't marry him."

Perry's laughter grated harshly. "She was goin' to wait till August. Then if you wasn't back Elkhart would put a ring on her finger—"

Alford stood rigid, his right hand hovering

above the butt of his gun. "She wouldn't marry him, I tell you!"

Clay Janner felt a vast pity for Joe Alford, then, and also a slight contempt. All eyes were on the man. Everyone in the saloon expected him to do something. He just stood there.

Clay shook himself. Not all men were proficient in the business of guns. Some men were scared. Baldy Renson had been scared. And if he let this thing go further Joe Alford would be lying dead on the cantina floor, probably before he got his gun out of leather.

"Your wife sure didn't pick much when she picked you," Perry said.

Alford said, "I won't stand for talk like that," and he tried to sound tough but failed to carry it off.

Lon Perry laughed again and Clay turned and looked at him. He considered how much he had at stake: a herd of Mexican cattle. And this yellow-haired gunman was threatening to wreck the game. He knew the setup here. The moment he or Alford tried to cut down on Lon Perry, the four Elkhart men outside would be at their backs.

Clay put his back to the bar. He saw that Leo Reese and Tom Shanley had come to stand beside Buck Bogarth. Clay gave them a long look, then let his gaze flick significantly to the street where the four Arrow men stood on the walk, all bending forward, elbows out and fingers hooked.

Bogarth licked his lips. "I want no part of this," he said, and jerked his head at Reese and Shanley. "Let's get out of here, boys."

As they shuffled for the door Alford looked stricken. "Wait—"

Clay clamped a hand on his partner's wrist. "Let them go," he said. "If they don't have guts enough to take chips in this game we're better off without them."

Fierro jerked hard at one of his spiked mustaches. "You go also, Senor Janner," he whispered across the bar to Clay. "Por favor. It will be the great favor."

But Clay ignored the Mexican and let his flat gaze flick over the remaining customers. Drifters, for the most part; save for a runty drummer with a sample case upended in a chair. Clay's eyes surveyed the room and they signaled their warning: Keep out of this.

He began to walk leisurely toward Perry's end of the bar. Four feet from the man he drew up. "You talk big," he drawled. "Mighty big."

"You fightin' Joe Alford's battles?" Perry said.

"Why not? He's my partner."

Perry laughed and slapped the bar top with the flat of his hand. The sound caused the drummer to jerk to his feet and upset his sample case. A profusion of corsets of varying sizes and hues fell from the sprung lid.

Perry's amusement ended abruptly. He looked toward the street, as if to see if his men were ready, then turned back to Clay. "Maybe you better tell Alford the real reason you feel sorry enough for him to fight his battles."

"You tell me," Clay said.

"It's on account of his wife. Reckon she asked you to the other night. Asked like only a woman can." He gave Clay a knowing smile. "Reckon you know what I mean Janner."

Clay heard Alford mutter an oath behind his back. He made a signal for Alford to keep out of it. Along the far wall the other customers had lined up, jaws slack, mouths open, knowing the danger from possible flying lead, yet unwilling to seek safety and miss the show.

Clay checked the window again. The four Arrow men stood rigid, their faces tight with rage. They stood with hands lifted shoulder

143

high. Across the street some passerby had come to a halt to stare. At first Clay couldn't understand what had happened. Then he saw that the Elkhart men, so confident that Bogarth and the other pool ranchers were out of the fight, had let themselves be taken from behind. Bogarth, Reese and Shanley were holding guns on the Arrow riders.

Perry evidently had not noticed any shift in the odds against him, for his insinuating voice droned on: "—You and Nina Alford was playin' it cozy in the cottonwoods the other night—" His voice broke off suddenly as he happened to glance at the window. He saw his men standing under the guns of the pool ranchers, and the sight stunned him.

Finally Perry tore his eyes from the window. Clay Janner rammed his gun muzzle into Perry's middle. The impact knocked the breath out of him. Clutching his stomach, he pitched to the floor, gagging and retching. Clay watched him without sympathy.

11

AN awesome silence hung over the cantina, broken only by the choking sounds Lon Perry made as he writhed in agony on the hard-packed dirt floor. The struggle for oxygen had put a tinge of purple on his features. Along the wall the drifters and the corset drummer seemed to be straining at invisible tethers. They showed a frantic urge to flee possible danger, yet this sudden degradation of the vaunted Perry held them for the finish.

Holstering his gun, Clay stepped back. "I'm waiting," he told the Arrow foreman. "If you've got the guts let's finish this."

With a low oath Perry struggled to his feet. He was still hunched over but some of the congestion had left his face. "Another time," he gasped, and started for the door.

Clay blocked him.

"Apologize," he said. "You made a reference to Mrs. Alford and me. Say it was a lie."

"But what if it ain't?" Perry was getting his

wind back, and with it his confidence. . . But when he glanced at the window and saw his four men still with their hands in the air, it seemed to put caution in him.

Before he could speak, Clay slapped his gaunt face. Perry yelled, and Clay hand-whipped him against the bar and then to his knees. Grabbing him by the shirt, Clay jerked him up again and held him close.

"You ever open your mouth again about Nina Alford," he said, "I'll kill you."

He flung Perry back against the bar. Slowly the man lifted a hand to his cheeks, mottled from the slapping Clay had given him.

"There'll be another day," he said.

"This is today," Clay said. "Now apologize, damn you."

Muscles bunched along Perry's swelling jaw. His eyes flared with a wildness, an urge to draw his gun. Quickly it died. "I—apologize," he said.

Perry wheeled for the door. Clay caught him and drew his gun and pushed him on out into the street. A crowd had gathered at a safe distance. Clay stepped behind the four Arrow men and pulled their revolvers from leather.

"We'll leave your guns in Fierro's," Clay told

146

them. He jerked his head at Buck Bogarth. "Find their horses, Buck. They've likely got rifles. Bring 'em here."

Later, the town stared in disbelief at the ignominy of the hand-picked Arrow crowd riding out of town without their guns. None of the Elkhart bunch looked back. At the edge of town they put spurs to their horses and rode at a dead run in the direction of Arrow.

Clay carried the weapons into the cantina and placed them on the bar. The place crackled with excited talk. Everybody was discussing the humiliation of Lon Perry, giving Clay sidelong glances.

"I wouldn't want to be in your boots, Mister," the drummer said as he stuffed corsets back into his sample case.

Clay ignored him. Now that it was over he felt a tremor in his thighs. Why had he done such a fool thing? What was Nina Alford to him? A woman who wasn't worth defending. . . .

Buck Bogarth came in with Shanley and Leo Reese. Bogarth was grinning, pleased with himself. "They figured we was ridin' out with our tails between our legs," the thick-necked

147

rancher said. "They was some surprised when they felt guns at their backs."

Clay said nothing. He noted that Joe Alford hadn't moved from the spot where he had been standing all during the trouble with Perry. Clay poured a drink, held it out to Alford, but the big redhead pretended he didn't see it. He started talking with Bogarth, discussing the reason the pool meeting had been called.

"Elkhart sent word he'll open his fence if we pay him two bits a head for all the beef we drive through," Bogarth said.

"Why don't he use a gun on us?" Tom Shanley said, shaking his gray head. "Either way it's a holdup."

"After us sidin' Clay Janner," Leo Reese said soberly, "I don't reckon Elkhart will deal with us at all."

Tom Shanley gave Bogarth a long look. "It was your idea to throw down on them Arrow men outside. What's Ardis goin' to say when she finds out you practically spit in Elkhart's face?"

Bogarth ran a thick finger back and forth along the wet bartop. "A man can't let his wife run him forever," he muttered.

"Big talk," Leo Reese said. "Wait'll you get home."

"Well, what the hell you expect us to do!" Bogarth burst out.

Leo Reese slapped the bar with the flat of his hand. "I'm glad to see you got a little fight left in you, Buck. Let's keep the pressure on Elkhart. What've we got to lose?"

Bogarth seemed to deflate, sighing, like a balloon. "If I was a single man, I'd say you was right. But—"

Reese came up to him on his bowed legs. "I'm married, Buck. I got as much to lose as you have."

"But your wife ain't like Ardis," Bogarth said weakly.

"I thought you was just through sayin' that a man can't let his wife run him forever."

Bogarth jerked down the brim of his hat, glared at Leo Reese, then shook an accusing finger at Clay. "This whole mess is your fault, Janner—and yours, Alford. Why in hell didn't you stay to home instead of leavin' your wife alone all them months so's Elkhart would figure—"

"You better shut up, Bogarth," Clay warned quietly.

Bogarth turned red, hitched up his pants and went storming outside.

There was a moment of silence in the cantina. Then Tom Shanley said, "Reckon all we can do now is play Elkhart's game. Two bits a head or drive across the Sink. Without Bogarth to string along with us we got no chance."

He clumped outside. After an awkward pause Leo Reese shrugged and followed him.

"There goes the end of the pool," Clay said, but Joe Alford didn't reply. He seemed busy cleaning his nails with the point of a knife.

Fierro leaned across his bar, his black eyes intent on Clay's face. "This I do not have the opportunity to say," he said in Spanish. "But the sheriff yesterday ask if I have seen you with this Baldy Renson the Senor Perry mentioned. The sheriff said that you are the class of man who could murder somebody like Renson."

Clay felt a slight chill at the back of his neck. "And where is our estimable sheriff today?"

"He is away on a matter of the tax," the Mexican said.

Clay gave him a slap on the arm. "You've gone out of your way to befriend me. Why?"

The Mexican stepped back, shrugging. "Some men you like. Some you don't."

150

Clay gave him a salute, then jerked his head at Alford. "Let's go before Elkhart comes riding in with a couple of ropes."

Outside in the bright New Mexican sunshine, Alford looked pale. They got their horses and started for Spade. As they climbed into the hills, Clay said, "You've got something on your mind, Joe. Spit it out."

They drew rein. The wind whipping up the pass stirred the ragged ends of Joe Alford's red hair. Alford seemed intent on studying the distant peaks of the Sabers, purple now against the sky.

"Don't tell me you believe Perry's lying tongue, Joe."

"Maybe you got a different story about what happened between you and Nina," Alford said grimly.

They were halfway down a narrow trail that bisected a rock-strewn canyon. Clay debated whether to tell Alford the truth. Then, knowing he would probably find out from the same informant who had given the information to Perry, he recounted Nina's visit to the cotton-woods. "She only talked about you, Joe. She wanted to know the truth about what happened in Mexico."

"You tryin' to say she'd believe you, instead of her own husband?"

Clay saw the wildness in Alford's eyes. Nothing else had seemed to rile the man, but now he was wound tight. He didn't want Alford maybe drawing a gun on him. He didn't want to be forced to shoot the big redhead.

Clay chose his words carefully. "Nina wanted to be sure, is all. She's been under a strain while you've been gone—"

Alford gave a short laugh. "Strain, hell. She was figuring to marry Elkhart if I'd stayed away four more months."

Clay said, "You should have had me write a letter, Joe. I didn't know you couldn't write. That's no disgrace."

"I wish I'd never met up with you that day in Paso," Alford said. "You talked me into this—"

Clay swung his horse in beside Alford's steel-dust. "Let's have it out," he said. "We've got too much tied up in that herd to let a lot of loose talk ruin us."

"I wish I'd never heard of Monjosa or them damn guns—"

"Maybe I do too. But it's over and done." He pounded his fist on the saddle-horn for emphasis. "There's nothing between me and Nina. You've got to believe that, Joe. If you never believe anything else in your life."

"Then why'd she have to sneak down and warm your blankets?"

"You're acting like a kid," Clay said—and found himself wondering if Alford ever would reach maturity.

"And why wasn't you sleepin' in the bunkhouse? Unless you knew Nina was comin' to meet you—"

"That's enough, Joe. I've had enough."

"And how'd Lon Perry get wind about you and Nina, anyhow?"

"Simple. Elkhart's got a spy in your outfit. How else?"

"Nina hired the new crew," Alford said, his lips curling. "Claimed the old bunch wouldn't leave her alone. I wonder."

"You better learn to trust her."

"You ain't one to trust a woman. If you was how come you never took a wife?"

"Never found the right woman." Again Clay beat his fist against the saddle-horn, once, decisively. "I've changed my mind. About a lot of things."

Alford regarded him narrowly. His face was

flushed. "Maybe you found the right woman now. My wife."

"If you weren't my partner," Clay said, "I'd gunwhip you out of the saddle."

Alford sat stiffly, right hand near his gun, as if daring Clay to make good his threat. Then the old fear seemed to eat in him and he dropped his hand. "Sometimes I ain't got the guts of a rabbit." He licked his lips as if they were dry. "But one of these days I'm goin' to get my nerve back, Clay. You say I got a cat on my back. Funny, but when I try to remember how my pa looked with that bullet in him—And me layin' there with a hole in my chest—it ain't so clear in my mind like it once was. Don't push me too far, Clay."

"I won't push you, Joe. For a lot of reasons. One of them being you saved my neck down in Mexico."

"If I had it to do over—" Alford broke off, swore, and resumed viciously. "Maybe I should've let that boy cut his initials on your chest with that saber." He neck-reined his horse and set it at a gallop for Spade.

At the house, Alford caught his wife alone. He told her about the tense scene at the cantina.

154

"Perry sure figures you and Elkhart was goin' to get married," he said.

Tears of anger sprang into her eyes. "Don't forget this, Joe. I could have married him in the first place. Instead I chose you." Her lips trembled. "Joe, I took you back. I'm your wife again. Why do you want to drag all this up?"

He seemed not to hear her. He stood in the parlor beside the Franklin stove, staring out into the empty yard. "How do I know what went on here while I was gone."

"I don't like this talk, Joe."

He turned on her. "You was goin' to marry Elkhart. You can't deny that."

She clasped her hands under her breasts. "Yes, I planned to marry him. I'd like to say I was going to marry him because I thought as his wife I'd be able to bring peace to this country. But I won't lie to you. The real reason was that I was tired of living alone. Tired of running a ranch. I'm not as young as Kate French. She's stood it so far but in five years she'll be an old woman. A woman can't take that sort of life. She needs a man."

"You sure needed a man," Alford said. "Elkhart."

Again she tried to make him listen to reason.

"We're together again, Joe. Clay convinced me that you and he really were in prison—"

"He convinced you mighty quick." Alford looked her over. She was small, defiant, her blonde hair loose about her shoulders. He sneered. "Maybe you and Clay—"

"Don't say it!"

"What about you and him in the cotton-woods?"

She swallowed. So they had been seen after all. "I wanted to get him out of here, Joe. That's the only reason I went out there. I threatened to tear my clothes—because I thought he would ride instead of risking a gunfight with his friend, his partner."

For a long time Alford stared at the reddish hairs on the backs of his big hands. Then he said, "I guess comin' home and finding Elkhart here has made me crazy jealous of every man."

"Jealousy can be a terrible thing, Joe. A man can lose his friends and his wife."

He sighed heavily. "Why ain't I good with a gun?" he wondered aloud. "Why can't I stand up to a man like Lon Perry when he insults my wife, instead of letting Clay—"

Nina's hand flashed to her mouth. "Clay took my part in town?"

156

"Yeah."

She turned quickly so he couldn't see the rush of color to her cheeks. Why did she feel so flustered? So Clay Janner had stood up for her. What of it?

"I wish to hell Clay could find some gal and settle down here," Alford said. "I'll feel lost when he pulls out."

"A lot of people will feel lost," she heard herself say.

"I got to make it up to Clay. I said some things I'm sorry for." He picked his hat off the steer-horn hatrack.

When he went out she stood woodenly, staring at the floor, her heart pounding. What was it about Clay Janner that stirred her? Was it the man himself, or was it only because he offered such a contrast to Joe? A strong, decisive man who'd know how to handle a woman. A man who would give a woman so much rein and no more. A man who would make the decisions, who wouldn't flounder around and let somebody else stick up for his wife. . . .

She walked to her room and closed the door and leaned against it. "Why did he have to come here?" she whispered. "Why?"

12

USUALLY Nina Alford did the cooking for the ranch hands, but with the six additional men Clay and Alford had brought with them the chore proved to be too much. The black-bearded Sam Lennox took over in a lean-to that adjoined the bunkhouse. All afternoon Clay avoided Russ Hagen, but during the evening meal in the bunkhouse he found Hagen watching him covertly from under his shaggy brows.

"I had to take care of a friend of yours today," Clay said abruptly.

Hagen rubbed a hand across his broken nose. "Who?" he demanded suspiciously.

"Lon Perry."

Russ Hagen's heavy shoulders stiffened. "Nobody in this country is that big."

"I slapped the hell out of him," Clay said, and broke a piece of cornbread into his beans.

The other hands stopped eating. Sam Lennox had come to the door of the cookshack, a dirty towel around his waist.

"You wouldn't be here talking about it," Hagen said, "if you'd really slapped Perry." Hagen gripped the edge of the table in his big hands. "You'd now be dead."

"Ask Fierro at the cantina. Or any one of twenty men."

A flicker of doubt showed in Hagen's close-set eyes.

Clay stirred the cornbread into his beans. The silence stretched thin in the bunkhouse.

Then Hagen asked his question. "How come you tangled with Perry?"

"I made him apologize for the filthy talk you spread about Mrs. Alford and me."

Hagen tilted his big head to one side. "You can prove I spread that talk?"

"I don't have to prove it. It's written on your face!"

Boots clattered as the crew quit the benches and ranged along the wall.

Hagen laughed. In the late afternoon sunlight seeping through the bunkhouse windows he looked formidable. On his thick upper lip, sweat gathered at a small scar, a memento of some forgotten brawl.

"All right," Hagen said, "I did see you and Nina Alford. You goin' to deny you and her was out back in the trees the other night?" He jerked a stubby thumb over his shoulder in the direction of the cottonwoods.

Clay's hand shot across the table. His fingers caught the front of Hagen's shirt. At the same moment Hagen lurched to his feet, tipping the table over on Clay.

But Clay had been waiting for this move and he leaped from the bench. The overturning table barely missed crushing his feet. As Hagen leaped across the table, aiming a blow for Clay's face, Clay hit him solidly on the neck. Hagen dropped into the wreckage of the table. But before Clay could get set, he was springing up, moving fast for his tremendous bulk. His large hands caught Clay at the shoulders, tried to drag him to the floor where his extra weight would tell. But Clay's right fist crashed against Hagen's eye. His left struck the big man on the point of the jaw. Hagen reeled. The crew yelled encouragement to Clay.

As Clay came in Hagen suddenly picked up a bench and hurled it. Clay tried to duck but the heavy bench caught him on the thigh and knocked him sprawling. Hagen leaped forward, intending to bring his boots crashing down on Clay's head. Had they landed, the man's weight

160

might have caved in Clay's skull, but the awesome possibility gave Clay an added strength. He jerked his head aside. Hagen struck the floor so solidly that it shook the windows. On one knee, Clay caught Hagen by a leg and threw his weight against it.

With a yell of rage and pain Hagen fell. He kicked free of Clay's grip, got to his feet. He saw a water pitcher and some glasses ranged on a shelf. He tried to grab the pitcher but Clay crashed into him. The shelf came down smashing the pitcher and the glasses on the floor. As the crew shouted and stomped the floor, the two men wrestled back and forth across the room, the cords in their necks standing out, faces bathed in sweat.

Then Clay slipped on a wet spot where coffee had been spilled. He tried to grab the front of Hagen's torn shirt in order to save himself from a fall. Hagen saw his advantage and with a scream of triumph managed to get both hands around Clay's neck.

A great roaring swept through Clay as Hagen's thumbs bore down on his windpipe with crushing force. He felt light in the head and he saw Hagen's crazy grin through a curtain of misty red. Hagen was shouting, laughing. He could feel the man's spittle against his cheeks. Desperately he struck with elbow and the heel of his hand. But Hagen covered up, keeping his chin on Clay's breastbone. Still the murderous pressure increased.

As if from a great distance Clay heard the voice of Sam Lennox: "Get him, Clay. Use your knee!"

This he did, but Hagen pulled back his body and the knee only brushed the big man's thigh. Just as he thought he might faint from the pressure, Clay gave a mighty wrench of his body. It was enough to break the hold. As he stepped back, trying to clear his vision, Hagen tore after him. Clay felt a shuddering smash at his jaw. For an instant there seemed to be no bone left in his legs. He staggered back. He saw Hagen come in, big arms flailing. In his eagerness Hagen left himself exposed. Clay brought up his right. It missed Hagen's jaw, but exploded with such force on the man's ear that he went to his knees.

"Finish him, Clay!" someone yelled.

With the numbing pain still at his throat, Clay lunged forward. One of Hagen's square, blunt-fingered hands groped for the handle of the shattered water pitcher. Clay saw the jagged

162

edge of glass reaching for his face. As Hagen came off the floor, Clay ducked under the blow. But Hagen got his lifted knee into Clay's groin. Although it was a glancing blow Clay felt it to the back of his head. He drove a hard fist into the pit of Hagen's stomach, then hung on. They wrestled across the floor, almost tripping over the wrecked table.

They crashed into a chair and both fell heavily. Although dazed, Clay struck powerful blows at Hagen's midriff. The big man, lying prone, was trying to pin Clay, but the punishment Hagen took at his belt line drove him away.

When they both staggered to their feet Clay knew he did not have strength enough left to continue the battle for long. Hagen's superior weight was a crushing advantage. And Hagen wanted to finish it, desperately wanted to finish it. He came smashing in. His left fist scraped Clay's cheekbone. Clay regained his balance and got set. Hagen drew back his right fist for the one that would end it, and Clay struck him hard on the jaw. The blow drove Hagen against the wall. A board in the bunkhouse wall splintered as Hagen's broad back struck it solidly.

The big man seemed to hang there. Clay took

a deep breath, feeling pain along his ribs, tasting blood from a cut lip.

Hagen took a lurching step toward him. Clay felt a sharp panic. He thought, I haven't got strength enough left to fight him off. I can't . . . And then Hagen crumpled to the floor.

Clay felt hands that weighed a ton slapping him on the back. He knew they were yelling but he couldn't hear because of the roaring in his head. Then he saw Joe Alford in the bunkhouse doorway. Alford was staring down at the unconscious Hagen. Nina Alford was clinging to Joe's arm. She looked at Hagen, then lifted her eyes to Clay's battered face.

"You're hurt," she said, and started forward, but Alford said something to her. She turned and went toward the house. She began to run, and the last Clay saw of her, she was hurrying across the veranda and into the house.

Clay wiped his face on a bandanna. Alford pointed at Hagen.

"Is he the one that talked about you and my wife?"

"Yeah," Clay said, and smeared a torn shirt-sleeve across his cut lip.

Alford drew his gun. He ordered one of the men to throw a bucket of water on Hagen.

When Hagen stirred and sat up, Alford said, "Get out, Hagen. If you set foot on Spade again, I'll kill you."

Still apparently dazed, Hagen reeled to his bunk, gathered up his things and went outside. Nobody saddled his horse or helped him in any way. When he finally rode out, he shook his fist at the bunkhouse. Then he was gone.

Alford holstered his gun. He and Clay were alone in the yard. Alford said awkwardly, "Looks like you're always fightin' my battles for me, Clay."

"Somebody had to settle with Hagen," Clay said, and nodded at Alford's holster. "You pulled a gun on him, Joe. You better watch out or it'll get to be a habit."

Then he limped back into the bunkhouse. He ached all over and he wished fervently that he had sense enough to pack up and get out. The way Nina Alford had looked at him after the fight had raised goosepimples along his back.

The next morning Kate French rode over and found him in the yard. She studied his bruises critically but made no reference to them. She seemed cool, and the rush of warmth he'd felt when she rode in left him quickly.

"I hear you've accomplished quite a bit this week," she said thinly.

At first he thought she meant Baldy Renson. It was possible that his body had been found.

"You humiliated Lon Perry in town," Kate said. "Now he'll never rest unless he kills you. Or tries to. And then you beat up Russ Hagen—"

"You seem to know all about me," he cut in.

"One of my men was in town. Hagen was in the cantina vowing what he'll do the next time he meets up with you."

"He'll have his chance—if he wants it."

"Honestly, Clay!" She sounded exasperated. "Do you go out of your way to make enemies?"

"I'd get pretty thin from running," he said wearily, "if I worried about every man who threatens me."

"You sound almost arrogant."

Clay studied her. With her blue-black hair slicked back she looked young and fresh and pretty. Not the sort of girl who had handled a ranch alone since the death of her brother.

"I guess you don't think very much of me," he said with a short laugh.

Her blue eyes seemed puzzled. She said, "I could never like a man who brought nothing

166

but trouble to his friends," and because he was still regarding her intently she flushed and folded her arms across her breasts. "Maybe it would be better if you took your half of the herd and cleared out."

"I may have to," he said, thinking of Nina Alford.

Kate's lips trembled and it seemed to anger her for some strange reason that he even considered leaving. "I don't see why you ever had to come here in the first place!" Her voice was louder than necessary.

"Joe Alford's my friend," Clay said. "But he exaggerates like we all do sometimes. He said the graze here was good. We'd let our herd fatten up then drive it to the railroad." He scratched his ear. "And Joe also figured that with me along it would be easier to explain to his wife why he'd been gone so long. But what do I find when I get here? A dry year. And on top of that a wife who can't make up her mind whether she wants her husband or another man."

Some of the stiffness seemed to go out of Kate's shoulders. "I guess things haven't been very easy for you, at that. But don't blame

Nina. She'd make up her mind in a minute if Joe would behave like a man."

"Joe's done his part," Clay said, sticking up for his friend.

"He's so busy feeling sorry for Joe he hasn't time for anything else. I wish—oh, I wish he'd never even come to this country in the first place."

Same wish for both of us, Clay thought.

"Well, maybe your life will be a little easier if I pull out," he said.

"I don't know whether it would or not," she said, giving him a strange look. Then she stepped around him and hurried toward the house.

Nina Alford came out on the porch to meet her, and at that moment Clay made his decision.

13

THAT evening Clay told Alford what he had decided to do. They talked in the yard, well away from the noisy bunkhouse. Lights glowed softly in the main house while Clay recounted their harsh troubles to Alford.

"The drought and the fence are going to outlast the pool easy," he said. "Bogarth is going to go broke paying Elkhart's toll. But he'll please his wife that way and stay out of trouble."

Alford nodded grimly. "I'm with you, Clay."

Clay shook his head. "I'm going alone." He was sick of the whole business. "You drive with the rest of the boys across the Sink. Either that or pay toll to Elkhart. Or get yourself a lawyer and grow gray waiting for the court to rule on the fence."

Alford looked hurt. "I told you I was sorry, Clay. About saying you and Nina was—"

"It isn't that. I'm getting tired, Joe. Damned tired of the way things have been going."

"What you figure to do?"

"I'm going through that fence."

"Clay, you can't—"

"We'll split the herd and I'll take half the crew."

Alford sighed miserably. The moon was rising over the hills. Horses stomped in the corral. "Maybe the boys won't run that much risk," Alford said. "Bustin' through that fence can get a man killed."

"If they don't want to risk it," Clay said, "then I'll find men who will."

Although Alford tried to argue against him going it alone, Clay was adamant, and in the morning they started rounding up the cattle they had brought out of Mexico. They intended to make a gather at the Buttes, run through a final tally there, and divide the herd. Working alone, Clay found himself in a ravine some miles west of Spade, prodding a small bunch of the Chihuahuas that didn't want to be driven back to the holding ground.

The sudden appearance of a rider on a bluff caused him to jerk his rifle from the boot. He swung down, levering in a shell as the rider came toward him. Then he saw that it was a woman. Nina Alford. He lowered the rifle and walked over to his horse and shoved the weapon into the scabbard.

"What're you doing here?" he demanded angrily. He scanned the ridges, wondering if she had been followed, but he saw no sign of movement.

She dismounted, trailed the reins. As she turned to unbuckle the straps of her saddlebags the sun brought out the lights in her blonde hair. From the saddlebags she removed a parcel wrapped in newspaper.

"I thought you might be hungry," she said. "Out here. Alone like this." She walked, swaying her body, to the shade of a juniper. There she sat down and opened the parcel. It contained two meat sandwiches. He thought of sending her on her way, but then he reconsidered. What the hell. He'd be gone from here in a day or so. He'd never come back. He sat beside her and took one of the sandwiches and began to eat.

"Joe says you're leaving," Nina murmured.

He nodded, his chinstrap swinging across the front of his faded shirt. "It's what you want, isn't it? Both you and Kate French."

She stiffened a little at mention of Kate. "I

never met a man like you, Clay," she said, and stared pensively at the ground.

"Men like me come pretty cheap in Texas," he said. Abruptly she leaned forward and placed the tips of warm fingers on the back of his hand. Her face glowed as she gazed at him. "I admit I didn't care for you at first, but—" A faint color spread across her cheeks when he made no move toward her. "Don't you like me at all?"

He wiped crumbs from his mouth, balled up the newspaper that had held the sandwiches and hurled it far down a gully. "You're another man's wife," he reminded her coldly.

"Where are you going, Clay, when you leave here?"

"After I sell the cattle I may go back to Mexico. Or maybe Montana. I hear there's good grass there. Without fences."

"What—" She shut her eyes tightly as if afraid to see his reaction to her words. "What if I wanted to go with you?"

He felt a tautness through his shoulders, and the sharp revival of an old hunger, but he waited it out behind a poker face. He watched a big Chihuahua steer nose out of the brush a hundred yards up the ravine. Overhead, a hawk dipped above the tawny crest of the rim. He got his breathing and his voice under control.

"I'll forget you said that," he said.

She drew back, her mouth bitter. "I don't want you to forget."

"Then look at it this way. Joe needs you."

"Joe needs a mother. He doesn't need a wife."

"You don't know Joe like I do," Clay said. "He worships you, Nina."

"But I don't *want* to be worshipped!"

"Look, Joe's lived a tough life. He never had much. I knew him years ago, remember. The kind of women he met, well, they weren't like you. Then he came to New Mexico and met you. He thinks you're better than he is. You've got an education. You own a ranch. Joe's been nothing in his life but a forty-dollar-a-month cowhand. But now he's got some cattle of his own. Why don't you give him a chance?"

"The chances are running out, Clay." She leaned close again. He could see a pulse in the white flesh at her throat, the thrust of her bosom against the cotton shirt. He didn't move.

"Why didn't Joe stick up for me?" she said petulantly. She sailed a couple of rocks down the ravine. "Lon Perry said—"

"Joe's gunshy now," Clay said. "But look out. One of these days he'll get over it. Don't egg him on until he makes a killer out of himself just to prove something to you."

"Nobody could push Joe that far. Nobody." She gave him a sulky sidelong glance. "I'm tired of things the way they are. Joe and I make up. And then he does some fool thing that turns me against him again. I'd like somebody to take care of me for a change. Really take care of me."

He rolled a cigarette because he could think of nothing more to say in Joe's defense.

Suddenly she flung herself across his lap and her shoulder knocked the half-finished cigarette out of his hands. He leaned back from her, bracing his body with his hands against the ground. They sat looking at each other a moment. He had an unholy urge to take his hands off the ground and grab her.

"I wonder if I ever loved Joe at all," she whispered.

"Sure you loved him. You still do." His voice had a sharp edge. "If you'll ever get some sense into that head."

"It's you I love, Clay."

"No."

"It must be you. Why else would I want to turn to you?" She lowered her eyes. "To go away with you."

"You'd be sick of me in a week."

She shook her head. "I love your strength. Because of what you did to Lon Perry, maybe."

A faint alarm touched him. High up on a hillside, a tiny spot of sunlight glinted on glass. Then it was gone. She shifted on his lap and her nearness made him forget anything else.

"You slapped Lon Perry's face," Nina said tensely. "Kate told me how you humiliated him. He'll never again be able to hold up his head around here. Without firing a shot you ruined the man."

"Somebody had to do it." He made a half-hearted effort to push her off his lap. Something he could have done easily with one hand, but didn't do because he lacked the will. In another minute . . . in one more minute. . . . Ah, but then, in the light of a hundred campfires in the years to come, he would see Joe Alford's face reflected there, and he would know what he had done to Joe.

There was a roaring in his ears as she pressed her mouth against his. But still he did not take his hands from the ground. She bit his lip lightly with her small teeth, then drew back, seeming unable to understand his lack of interest.

"You're not made of stone," she whispered. "Don't pretend that you are."

"No, I'm not made of stone," he admitted tensely. "You're going to make a fool out of yourself. Out of me. And when it's over you'll still be in love with Joe Alford."

"That's where you're wrong. So very wrong."

When she tried to claim him again he fended her off with a forearm. "I'm a stranger who came into your life at a time when you're having trouble with a husband." He made a cutting gesture with his hand. "It's happened plenty of times before. It'll happen plenty of times again."

She seemed angry and at the same time puzzled. "Clay, it's us. Together—"

His lip still throbbed from the bite she'd given him. He watched her eyes. They were very bright, and he knew he had to try once more. He said the first thing that came into his head. "How do you know I'm not in love with somebody else?"

She sat up abruptly and the brightness left her eyes. For an instant she seemed stunned. Then she cried, "It's Kate. You're in love with Kate French!"

He was startled to hear it thrown back at him like this. But, wanting to end it between them for good, he pressed on. "It had to happen sometime in my life," he said, very deliberately. "I'm glad it's Kate."

"Why, damn her, damn her, damn her!" Nina beat the ground with her fists. Then the rage was gone. She put a hand across her eyes, and wept, and her whole mood changed.

"I'm glad, Clay. Really I am. God knows Kate needs a man."

He didn't know what to say. He felt at a loss with a weeping woman on his hands. Nina dried her eyes on a bandanna she took from the pocket of her divided skirt.

"Maybe what happened out here today was good for me," she said. "I got something out of my system."

He helped her up. "It was worth it then," he said, but watched her warily. She was unpredictable.

"Did I make a fool out of myself, Clay?"

"Everybody does. At least once in a lifetime.

Now go home to—" His voice broke. Far up the slope, he had seen the crown of a man's hat briefly outlined against the junipers.

14

BECAUSE he said none of his men had the brains to track a five-legged cow through 'dobe mud, Byrd Elkhart hired Charlie Snow. Snow was a squawman who lived up on the Rim, raised a few horses and goats and hunted a little when he felt like it. For a time he had been an Army scout at Fort Ross. He was a graying, solid man who had lived so long among the Indians that strangers frequently mistook him for one. During the winter he wore a blanket over his shoulders and favored an old black slouch hat with a feather in it.

For extra money he sometimes hired himself out as a tracker. He had sharp black eyes wreathed in wrinkles at the corners from years of squinting at the ground to read sign.

This day Byrd Elkhart met him at Arrow and told him what he wanted done and Charlie Snow grunted and agreed to do the job for five dollars and a bottle of whisky. They started out at Squaw Creek where the stench from the slaughtered—and still unburied—Chihuahua steers was almost unbearable.

While Charlie Snow dismounted and prowled around, Elkhart sat easy in his saddle. So did Lon Perry. But Russ Hagen and three other Arrow men who had come along all dismounted and sought a tree to rest under.

Lon Perry removed his hat, smoothed his yellow hair and watched Charlie Snow bent over the ground, studying it with his wise old eyes. "If Charlie don't find Baldy," Lon Perry said to Elkhart, "there'll never be any finding him."

Elkhart paused in the act of lighting a cigar and glared at Perry. Without speaking he finished puffing the cigar alight. Perry looked at the rest of the crew, all sprawled in the shade, and then he reined his horse closer to Elkhart's pinto.

"Look, Byrd, there's no use bein' sore. I told you I lost my temper with that son—"

Elkhart's teeth clamped down on the cigar butt. "Dragging Nina Alford's name in like that. In a saloon. Lon, I ought to shoot you. Sure as hell I ought to."

Lon Perry sat very straight in the saddle. He put on his hat and said flatly, "Don't talk about shootin' people unless you mean it."

Because he wanted no more trouble on his hands than he had already, Elkhart pretended to back down a little. "I don't give a damn what you do to Clay Janner. But it can be done without bringing Nina into it."

"I'll take care of him, don't worry," Perry snapped.

Elkhart scanned his foreman's face. It was still puffy from the backhanding Clay had given him in the saloon. "You'll have to do better than you did the last time you met up with him," Elkhart said, because he just couldn't resist saying it.

Perry colored. "If he hadn't had that damn pool bunch at our backs we'd have finished him."

"*We'd* have finished him? How many does it take to put Janner in the ground? I thought you were tough enough to do it yourself, Lon."

"You tryin' to pick a fight with me?"

Elkhart gave a slight shrug. "I just don't like all these lies about Nina."

"They ain't lies."

Elkhart dropped his right hand to his gun. "Nina was never out in the cottonwoods with Clay Janner."

"But Hagen saw 'em—"

181

"And Hagen's a liar. How many times do I have to tell you?"

Hearing his name mentioned, Hagen jerked up his head. He sat a little apart from the three regular Arrow men. His face was so misshapen as to be hardly recognizable. One eye was still nearly closed. He had a cut on his jaw, and his knuckles were raw and swollen.

"I seen 'em," he said shortly. "Don't worry about that."

Elkhart started to rein his horse toward Hagen. The rawhide quirt which had been dangling by its wristlock flicked up into his hand. Lon Perry drove his dun in front of the pinto to block him.

"Don't do some damn fool thing you'll be sorry for, Byrd," Perry warned. "You got enough trouble without layin' the quirt to Hagen."

Elkhart pulled up, scowling, just as Hagen came to his feet. He thoroughly hated Hagen for spreading those lies about Nina. And he hated Lon Perry's part in the business at Fierro's. It was bad enough that the woman he intended marrying had been dishonored in a saloon. But his own foreman and his men had been made to look like a pack of fools. He'd gotten the whole story from some of the eye witnesses to the affair.

And on top of everything else Hagen had been soundly whipped by Clay Janner.

"I suppose when it comes down· to it," Elkhart muttered, "I'll be the one to handle Janner."

Charlie Snow grunted something, and that broke it up. As they followed Snow along a narrow trail Elkhart admitted that he welcomed the interruption. Perry had spoken one truth today, at least. He had enough trouble already without adding to the burden. He was glad he hadn't quirted Hagen.

Moving through the heat of the forenoon, Elkhart thought of how he would really make the basin ranchers crawl now. The hell with two bits a head toll. He would make it twice that— unless Nina agreed to quit stalling and kick Alford off the place and let him start the judge working on a divorce. If she keeps on, Elkhart thought grimly, she won't have to divorce Alford. She'll be a widow instead.

Several times on the trail Charlie Snow got down on his hands and knees, sniffing the ground like an old hound dog. Elkhart knew the trail was stone cold now, and no telling how many riders had been over this ground since the day Baldy Renson disappeared. His own men had covered it a dozen times, hunting for a trace of the missing rider. But if anybody could find sign on a cold trail, Charlie Snow could.

Shortly before noon Charlie Snow called another halt. He dismounted and sniffed around and then went off the trail a few steps and stood looking at something, arms folded, a faint grin of triumph on his lips.

Elkhart came up to stand beside him. Charlie Snow pointed at a pile of rocks. He stepped forward and began pitching the rocks aside. The waxy-dead face of Baldy Renson appeared, and then the whole body. Elkhart ordered it wrapped in a blanket.

"Take him to town, Charlie," Elkhart said, and dropped five silver dollars into Snow's outstretched hand. Then, thoughtfully, he added two more. "Take him to the sheriff. Maybe this'll get Bert Lynden off his dead ass."

"You promise whisky," Charlie Snow grunted.

"Get it from Fierro. Tell him to put it on my bill."

After the body was loaded and on its way to town, Elkhart took a deep breath. The stench here had been almost as bad as the dead-cow stink at Squaw Creek.

"Well, you got Janner right this time," Lon Perry said, grinning. "Let's go find him."

"Bert Lynden hasn't hung a man in a long time," Elkhart remarked. "About time he had a little practice."

"If Bert's got a weak arm," Perry said, "I'll work the trap lever myself. It'll be a pleasure. When Janner drops through the hole I'll spit in his face. That'll also be a pleasure."

"We haven't got him yet," Elkhart said.

"We'll get him."

Because one of the Arrow men had reported activity to the south on Spade range, the group headed that way.

Just past noon, as they were crossing a timbered ridge, Lon Perry pulled up. "Let me have a look through them glasses, Byrd."

He held out his hand. Elkhart rose in the stirrups and peered below. He saw nothing but a Chihuahua steer in the canyon. He removed a pair of field glasses from his saddlebags and handed them over to Perry.

Perry adjusted them to his eyes, then whistled softly. He lowered the glasses and gave Elkhart a long, speculative look.

Exasperated at Perry's behavior, Elkhart said, "What's down there?" He extended his hand for the glasses.

"This is something you won't want to see, Byrd."

"Give me those glasses." Elkhart took the glasses, and while he adjusted them, Lon Perry gave the order for the rest of the men to dismount.

Gradually, as he focused the glasses, the scene in the canyon came into Elkhart's view. He saw two saddled horses below, reins trailed. He shifted the glasses and caught his breath. He closed his eyes for a moment, then opened them. No, his vision wasn't playing tricks on him. Down in that canyon, Clay Janner was sitting on the ground. And Nina Alford was lying limp in his lap.

He felt a sudden tautness in his chest as if his heart had swelled and threatened to burst through his breastbone. He lowered the glasses, put them in his saddlebags. He swung down. He was very pale.

A faint, wicked grin started across Perry's lips. He caught himself and masked it. "Satisfied?" he asked softly.

186

Elkhart nodded. He didn't trust himself to speak.

"I told you the kind she was, Byrd."

Elkhart spun, jerking up his gun. "Goddam you, Lon," he said. Then he got hold of himself and holstered the gun. The men were looking on, owl-eyed. They did not know what was happening in the canyon below.

Elkhart cleared his throat. A vein pulsed at his forehead. "Nina Alford and Janner are down there," he said, jerking a thumb toward the canyon. "Let's get Janner."

"We don't have to wait for the sheriff," Lon Perry said, and unfastened his saddle rope.

"We'll handle this my way," Elkhart said. His lips thinned like a bloodless gash across his bloodless face. "Understand?"

Leaving one man behind to bring up the horses at a signal, the rest began to make their way down the slope.

15

THE instant Clay saw the crown of the hat against the hillside, it disappeared. The horses had caught a scent and were moving restlessly behind them. Clay whispered, "Get behind me, Nina," and the girl, frightened now, moved as he directed.

Before Clay could draw his gun, Lon Perry's voice reached him from the opposite side of the canyon. "Hold it, Janner. You don't want the woman hurt, do you?"

Clay felt a quick fear as he saw Perry standing not a dozen yards away holding a rifle. Perry stepped forward, and then the rest of the party came down into view. Clay saw Byrd Elkhart, and Hagen, his beefy face scarred from the fight in the bunkhouse. Two other men were with them. One of the men turned and shouted something toward the rim and in a moment a rider leading saddle horses started down a slanted trail.

Clay said, "Get your horse, Nina. Ride out of here. They won't stop you."

Nina was numb with terror. She stumbled toward her horse.

"You stay here," Elkhart ordered. His face was a stone mask of rage. "I want you to watch it," he added.

Slowly he paced across the canyon floor, his men spread out, each holding a gun. Elkhart came to a halt a few feet away and gave Nina a terrible smile. "Lon, if Janner makes a wrong move, shoot him. In the stomach."

"I hope he makes that move," Lon Perry said. "I'd like that."

Nina stepped in front of Clay. "Please, Byrd, you don't understand. Don't do anything to him. He talked sense to me about Joe. I—"

"I heard the sort of woman you are," Byrd Elkhart said. "I didn't believe it till now."

Nina went white. "Byrd, you misunderstand—"

"We watched you through field glasses," Elkhart said.

Clay swallowed. Field glasses. Sure, the reflection of sun on glass he had seen briefly.

Elkhart put out a thick arm, encircled Nina's waist and drew her against him. "I wait for you to make up your mind about Joe. And all the time it's Janner. I find you out in the brush with a range tramp like him." He gave an ugly laugh.

"Byrd, don't do anything you regret," Nina said. She tried to struggle but he held her too tightly.

"Get his gun," Elkhart ordered.

Clay felt sweat break out on the nape of his neck. He heard Perry come up behind him, felt the pressure of the rifle muzzle against his back. One of the Arrow men came around and lifted his revolver.

Elkhart said, "Remember what we did to the Mex we found with the running iron?"

Perry laughed softly. "Hell, you must really hate Janner."

"Don't you?"

"Yeah, a little," Perry drawled. "He mussed up my face. I'd like to take him to town and see him hang for killin' Baldy Renson—"

Clay stiffened.

"Yeah, we found his body," Lon Perry told him grinning a little. "But maybe this other will be better than a hanging. It'll last longer, that's for sure."

On Elkhart's order two of the men got saddle ropes and spun out loops. These they dropped over Clay's head, cinching them tight at the waist. Keeping the pressure on the ropes, the two men edged away from Clay, leaning on them as if holding a downed steer. Clay tried to tense his muscles to stave off the ropes cutting into his waist. He didn't have long to wonder what was happening next. He saw Nina, looking sick, Elkhart holding her with his arm, his eyes glittering. To one side, Russ Hagen stood with his big fists clenched, waiting.

Lon Perry suddenly reversed his rifle and struck Clay cruelly on the kidney. The force of the blow knocked him off balance. Because the two ropes held him tight, his feet went out from under him. He flung out his hands wildly to break his fall, but they did little good. He tipped forward, striking his head on the ground. Momentarily stunned, he dangled, feet in the air, while the two Arrow men sweated and dug their boot heels into the ground to keep him there.

"Hold him, boys!" Elkhart shouted. "Take a turn with him, Hagen."

Rubbing the raw knuckles of his hands, Hagen came lumbering up. He caught Clay by the hair, jerked him upright and smashed him in the face. The power of the blow knocked him backwards. Desperately he fought for balance, but pinwheeled between the ropes, striking the back of his head on the ground. He tried to right himself but Hagen came in and kicked him in the ribs. Pain and savage anger knifed through Clay. He tried to grab Hagen by a leg, but the big man only laughed and hit him again.

Clay sagged on the ropes, bent over, dazedly watching a bright pattern in the dust. He realized numbly that it was his blood. He was aware of Nina's screaming, but the sound barely penetrated the captive thunder that roared inside his skull.

They hauled him upright and when he tried to fight Hagen slashed him in the face. Again and again he tried to meet Hagen's rush, but each time the pair with the ropes jerked him off balance. Finally he went down hard. The world tilted at a crazy angle and seemed very strange like a place he had never seen before. They pulled him upright.

As he stood there, nearly out on his feet, he saw that Hagen and Lon Perry had mounted their horses. The ends of the two ropes were passed to them.

Perry lolled in the saddle, grinning. "How are you at running a footrace, Janner?"

Clay swayed, shaking his head, trying to clear it. His body was one big bruise. His head ached intolerably.

"That Mex ran pretty far that day," Elkhart said. "But he couldn't catch a horse. Too bad."

Nina tried to claw free of Elkhart's arm. "You'll kill him!" she sobbed.

"When we're through with him you can sit on his lap till there's four feet of ice in hell—"

"Please, Byrd," Nina begged. "Don't do this."

"I loved you for years, Nina," Elkhart said in a choked voice. "When you married Alford I gave up. Then when he went to Mexico and didn't come back I saw a chance. I even sent that man to you with Joe's watch so you'd think he was dead." He scowled down at her. "I wouldn't have you now. Not after finding you with a no-good like Janner."

"But you're wrong, Byrd. It wasn't like you thought—"

"I tell you I saw you through the glasses."

Clay gripped the two ropes, trying to ease the pressure at his waist. His ribs ached and the flesh at his waistline had been rubbed raw by the hemp. He saw big Russ Hagen sitting high in the saddle, and fifteen yards to his left, Lon Perry. They dallied the ropes around their saddle horns.

"Let's get movin'," Lon Perry said, and they started their horses down canyon at a walk.

Clay lurched along behind them, helpless, his throat dry. And in him the terror that comes with certainty of death began to grow. Here on this clear warm day they meant to kill him.

The pace increased and soon the horses were at a lope, hauling Clay at a run behind them. In his high-heeled boots on the uneven ground it was hard to maintain balance. Frantically he tried to keep up with them. He knew what would happen once the horses went into a gallop. He'd be forced to run faster and faster, fighting for balance. And finally he would lose it altogether.

A picture of a rider he had once seen dragged by a frightened horse flashed before his eyes. The rider's face had been unrecognizable, and so was the rest of him.

As he fought desperately to hang onto the ropes, he saw the spurs dig in. The horses jerked him into a dead run. His legs scissored in great frantic strides. Within a dozen yards he lost his grip on the ropes. It seemed that a great and sudden weight pressed at the back of his head, tipping him toward the ground. In another moment he would be pinwheeling at the end of the ropes. And that would send him crashing headfirst to the ground.

But then he saw Hagen rear up in the saddle. Hagen swayed, flung up his right hand high as if to peer at his armpit. A sudden wash of redness showed there, and the sharp crack of a rifle reached them. Hagen pitched loosely to the ground and his horse veered, pulling Clay off his feet. Before the horse could drag him it went down. Another rifle report reverberated in the canyon.

Shaken as he was, Clay managed to get to his knees. He stayed there, sobbing for breath. Lon Perry had reined in his own mount and was peering back down the canyon, back toward Elkhart and Nina. Hagen began to stir on the ground. The man sat up and stared dazedly at a bleeding right arm. He looked sick from bullet shock.

Gradually Clay's eyes focused. He saw Lon Perry raise his hands in the air. And there on the slope behind Perry was Sam Lennox. Sam, the black-bearded hand Clay had picked up at the border. Sam was holding a rifle on Lon Perry.

"Get on down there by Elkhart," Sam Lennox said and rode a dun horse out of the brush. He nodded at Clay. "You just set there, boss. We'll come back for you directly."

Clay saw Sam Lennox herding Lon Perry and the wounded Hagen on down the canyon. Hagen was riding double with Perry. He sagged in the saddle, holding his bad arm.

Now Clay could see that Elkhart had released Nina. The woman had quickly got away from him. The thing that surprised Clay the most was seeing Kate French standing behind Elkhart, a rifle trained on the man's back. Her face under the dark hair seemed very pale, but very firm.

"I hated to shoot a horse," Kate said, "but I wasn't going to stand by and see you drag Clay Janner to pieces."

Elkhart jerked around and glared at Kate. "You horning in like this, puts you on the other side of my fence. See that you stay there!"

Then Sam Lennox came up, herding Perry and the wounded Hagen. Elkhart shook his fist at Lennox. "I'll remember this day, friend. If you've got the brains of a gnat you'll clear out of New Mexico!"

"Unbuckle your gunbelt and shut up," Lennox ordered. "I oughta kill you for what you done to the boss."

Elkhart swore, but under the threat of the man's rifle he did as he was told. And in addition to Lennox there was Kate French standing there coolly with a rifle. And he seemed to know from the look in her eye that she wouldn't hesitate to shoot him.

Lon Perry, holding the wounded Hagen in the saddle in front of him, seemed reluctant to part with his gun. But at last he unfastened his gunbelt and let the rig fall to the ground. Lennox got his rifle from the boot and also Hagen's gun. Then he lifted a rifle from Elkhart's saddle.

"Janner got lucky today," Lon Perry told Kate. "His luck won't hold. Not worth a damn it won't!"

"Kate, you've only postponed the inevitable," Elkhart said. "Clay Janner will hang before the month is out!"

Hagen appeared to realize for the first time what was going on. Blood dripped off the ends of his fingers. He looked around. "You goin' to let 'em spoil our fun?" he demanded of Elkhart.

"Oh, God," Elkhart groaned. "Let's get out of here. If you lose that arm you can thank Kate French and her black-bearded friend!"

After that, Elkhart led his men up the slanting trail to the rim and then into the junipers. Only when the sound of their passing had faded did Kate lower her rifle. Her hands left streaks of moisture on the weapon.

"Thank God, Kate," Nina sobbed, finding her voice for the first time. "How in the world did you find us?"

"I rode over to your place today just as you left," Kate said. "I followed you. I hoped to keep you from doing something foolish with Clay Janner."

"You don't have to worry, Kate. Clay is—"

"Let's get him out of here," Kate said. They rode to the spot where Sam Lennox was tending Clay. Lennox had pulled the ropes off him. Clay's nose was smashed, his mouth cut. Kate shuddered at the marks of the beating.

"Thank God I had presence of mind enough to ask Sam Lennox to ride with me," Kate said. "I guess I was afraid to ride alone. This country isn't exactly the safest place for a woman."

Clay said, "You get back to the ranch, Sam. I'll be along directly."

"You all right, boss?" Lennox said anxiously.

Clay nodded. Lennox argued that he should stick around, but Clay was worried about the herd. Elkhart would move fast now.

After Lennox left, Kate gave Clay a severe look. "What if Joe Alford finds out you were here with Nina today?"

"He'll find out," Clay said, and every word sent a vibrating jolt of pain up into his broken, blocked nose. "Elkhart will spread the word."

"Then get out of the country," Kate said. "Before you and Joe get into a gunfight over this."

Clay shook his head, took a step toward his horse, and passed out cold.

16

CLAY was awakened by the murmur of voices. He jerked up his head, grimaced with pain. He closed his eyes, then opened them again, surprised to find he was in a bedroom. There were curtains at the windows. A woman's scent lingered in the room. He stirred in the big bed where he lay and realized that cool sheets touched his bare skin. He managed to get to his elbows. His clothing lay on a chair.

The voices came nearer. Kate French entered the room. An old man followed her in. Clay pulled up the blankets, feeling embarrassed at his nakedness.

"Clay, this is Charlie Snow," Kate said. "He wants to talk to you."

Clay nodded at the old man but looked at Kate. It was the first time he had ever seen her in a dress. She seemed younger, more feminine. Pretty, by God. She must have sensed his interest, for her dark blue eyes showed pleasure.

She went out, closing the door. Charlie Snow padded up on his moccasins. "Ain't got but a minute, Janner. I'm headin' out. So you pay attention. Elkhart hired me and I done what he paid me for—"

"I don't understand," Clay said.

Snow lifted a wrinkled brown hand. "When Elkhart first settled in these parts a lot of my wife's people still lived here. Them he couldn't run off, he killed. I been waitin' years to get even with him. So—"

Kate rushed into the room. "Clay, Joe Alford is outside! He's drunk and wearing a gun!"

"Send him in. I'll talk sense to him."

"You can't talk sense to a crazy man. Elkhart has spread a vile story about you—" She broke off, glancing at Charlie Snow's impassive, leather-brown face.

"I heard all about it," Snow said. "It's another thing I got against Elkhart. What he can't have himself, he'll ruin for everybody else."

Clay sat up in bed, and the covers fell away from his bare chest. "Kate, get me a gun."

Charlie Snow padded to the door. "I'll go and try to get him to cool his ornery temper."

He went out. Clay started to climb out of the

bed, then ducked back under the covers. Kate smiled faintly. His face flamed as he considered the implications.

"Don't worry," she said. "I didn't undress you. A man did."

When she left the room he frowned at her manner. She seemed so completely different. Mellow. His stiffened fingers fumbled at buttons. His head ached and his whole face seemed to be one big bruise. A mirror above a chest of drawers caught his eye. Studying his reflection, he wondered if he would ever look the same again. His nose had a dent in the midst of its swollen mass. The cuts on forehead and cheeks, doctored with arnica, might leave scars.

He buckled on his gunbelt, glanced at his empty holster. Then he went searching for Kate. He heard the muffled clop-clop of horses moving out of the yard.

Outside, he found Joe Alford face down in the dirt. There was a gash on the back of Alford's head. A gun lay near his outstretched fingers. Some of Kate's riders were squatting on their heels, surveying the prone exhibit with solid satisfaction. Kate put them in motion with a crisp order.

"Get him to the bunkhouse," she said. "Tie him down until he sobers up."

She turned to Clay, looking scared. "He was going to shoot you on sight. Charlie Snow got behind him and hit him."

Clay teetered numbly on his trembling legs. He looked around the yard. "Where is Snow?"

"He left. Heading south with his wife into the Mogollons where Elkhart can never find him."

Clay fingered his chin and winced. "What in hell was he trying to tell me in the house?"

"Something about a man named Baldy Renson," Kate said. "That's all I know. Clay, you should get back to bed and save your strength."

"Baldy Renson," Clay murmured, and felt a chill in the pit of his stomach. "I've got to get out of here!"

Kate's men carried Joe Alford off to the bunkhouse. Now Clay and Kate were alone in the yard. She tried to argue him into staying. He wouldn't hear of that, but he did agree to let her cook him a meal.

In the big kitchen of the ranch house she fried him a steak and eggs and plied him with black coffee laced with whisky. The meal and the coffee helped stir life into him once again.

"I sort of got off on the wrong foot with you, Kate," he said. "I'm glad we're friends now."

"So am I," she said, and blushed. She sat across from him at the table. She had gotten a revolver and given it to him. The gun had belonged to her brother. Armed again, he felt almost whole.

But something in Kate's eyes disturbed him. She seemed to be searching his face for the answer to an unvoiced question.

"I'm not very pretty," he said, and ran a hand over his bruised jaw.

"I don't care what you look like," she whispered.

A sense of panic swept over him, as he felt invisible bonds tightening. This was no time to become involved with a girl. He sat up straighter and reached for the bottle and poured more whisky into his coffee. His head was swimming pleasantly, but he knew he had to end this thing now.

"How'd you get me here?" he asked. "I don't remember anything."

"Nina and I held you in the saddle."

"Nina's a lonely woman," he said, and forced

a laugh. "Why, for a while she figured she wanted to run off with me. That shows how crazy a woman can get."

"I know," Kate agreed. "All women are a little crazy when it comes to some certain man."

He felt the panic mount. "I made Nina come to her senses. Not that she wouldn't have anyway, but—" He looked away. "Well, I told her I was in love with you. I hope you don't mind, Kate."

"So she said," Kate snapped, and got to her feet. "No, I don't mind if you'd lie about a thing like that." Her voice trembled. "Any lie is sufficient if it'll save a woman from making a fool of herself."

She started to leave the room, but he came out of the chair and caught her by a wrist. She yanked hard and freed herself. "I won't stand for you manhandling me like you did that day at Spade!"

"Kate, I—" His brain whirled dizzily and he supposed it was due to the pounding he had taken that day. Or was it something else? He heard himself say, "Kate, maybe if I'm lucky and can sell my half of the herd—"

"You can go to Montana," she said icily. "There's free grass and no woman to tie you down." She rubbed her wrist as if she were wiping off something his fingers had left. "I understand there's a cattle buyer in Reeder Wells looking for beef. His name is Ruskin. Maybe you can make a deal with him."

Then she whirled, her skirts whipping about her legs. As she fled the room he had an impression of inswept waist, of full hips undulating. At the door she paused to look back at him and he saw the heaving upthrust of her breasts. Her eyes were wet. Then she was gone, slamming the door behind her.

"Kate!"

He started after her, then stopped. He thought: This is what you want, damn it. Isn't this what you've always wanted? On the move. Take your fun, make a little money, spend it.

Snatching the bottle of whisky from the table, he went to the bunkhouse. Kate's crew were lolling around, talking about Joe Alford and all that had happened. Alford lay roped to the bunk. He was conscious. As Clay came up he saw the intense hatred in Alford's eyes.

"Listen, Joe," Clay said, "you've got to believe—"

Alford called him a name Clay would never

have taken from another man. White-faced, he handed the bottle to one of Kate's men.

"Give him this bottle," he said. "When it's empty, give him another. It's the only thing he's got left. He hasn't got the guts to fight for his wife. He hasn't got the guts to fight for his pride or for anything."

He went out into the yard and with his sore and aching fingers he managed to saddle his horse. Then he rode for Reeder Wells and he didn't look back. If he had, he would have seen Kate French at the window.

17

BYRD ELKHART glared across the small jail office at Bert Lynden. The sheriff squirmed in his swivel chair, his fleshless face losing color under the rancher's burning gaze. The air in the room smelled stale, musty. In better years a deputy kept the office open, but recently the county had seen fit to keep the place closed, save for the periods when Lynden came down from the county seat.

"Bert," Elkhart said, "who put you in office?"

"You did, Byrd, but—"

"Then I'm entitled to some consideration for my support."

Lynden got to his feet, holding out his thin hands imploringly. "Byrd, I swear to God I ain't seen Charlie Snow."

"If you're lying to me, so help me I'll run you clear to Chihuahua!" Elkhart took a threatening step toward Lynden. "Charlie Snow was supposed to bring in Baldy Renson's body. Now where is it?"

Lynden looked completely bewildered. "There's no body in the shed out back of the hotel. You looked there yourself. And I haven't seen Charlie Snow in a year."

"Last time I saw Snow he had Renson's body roped to a horse—" Elkhart stiffened as something clicked at the back of his mind. "By God," he whispered hoarsely.

"You figure maybe Snow double-crossed you?" Lynden said hopefully, as if this would direct Elkhart's wrath to other quarters.

"I just remembered something. Years back he threatened to get even with me—" Elkhart broke off, clenching his fists.

"Even with you for what, Byrd?"

"When I first came here there were some Indians camped at Squaw Creek and I . . . well, how the hell did I know one of 'em was a woman?"

"So that's how the creek got its name," Lynden murmured, and then wisely shut up.

"Is there a law, Bert," Elkhart asked with deceptive mildness, "that says you can't hang a squawman to a tall tree?"

He started for the door, but Lynden managed to get there first and block him. "Now looky here, Byrd," the sheriff said with unaccustomed fervor, "you can't go around hanging people."

"Don't tell me what to do," Elkhart said. He caught the sheriff by a shoulder and tried to push him away from the door. Lynden held his ground. Elkhart stepped back, resting a hand at his gun.

"You really bracing me, Bert?"

Lynden shook his head. He was scared and he showed it. But also there was a new defiance in him, defiance born of desperation.

"I'll play your game, and you know it," he said. "But I also got my own hide to look out for. You've stirred up too big a mess with that damned fence of yours, Byrd."

"You know something you haven't told me?"

Lynden mopped his wet forehead. "Just before I left the county seat I got a letter from the governor's office. Seems somebody wrote him about your fence. Claimed you blocked off a legal right-of-way through the mountains. The governor, he told me to look into it."

Elkhart scowled. "Why didn't you tell me?"

"I figured you'd work something out with that basin crowd and I wouldn't have to."

"You're getting damn ethical all of a sudden," Elkhart said heavily. "And in the line of duty I demand that you swear out a warrant for Clay Janner. For murder."

The sheriff spread his hands. "You show me Baldy Renson's body and I'll do it, Byrd. But I'm not going to make a fool of myself—"

Elkhart shoved him roughly away from the door. "You'll have a body," he said. "I'll bring in Baldy Renson. Or I'll bring in Charlie Snow and he'll talk or I'll burn the hide off his Indian feet."

Elkhart stormed out of the jail office, walked down to Fierro's and shouted at his men. Lon Perry and three Arrow riders headed out of town for the high mountains where Charlie Snow maintained his camp. Russ Hagen, getting his arm bandaged at the doctor's office, watched them ride out.

It was dark when Clay arrived in town. From the shelter of the Mercantile he gave the short business block a close scrutiny, but he saw no sign of the Arrow crowd. Satisfied, he racked his horse and got the proprietor of the Mercantile to keep his place open until he could purchase a new shirt, pants and underwear. After changing his clothes and discarding the garments torn and bloodied in the fight in the canyon, he went to Fierro's.

There were six men in the saloon and from the way they looked at his bruised face Clay knew they had heard the story.

Fierro set out a bottle and gave one of his spike mustaches a tug. "It is good that you are alive, senor."

Clay poured a drink and said in a voice loud enough for all to hear, "Nina Alford's a good woman. You remember that."

Fierro nodded. "I remember."

"Then remember this too. I'll kill the man who says different." Clay had his drink and the straight whisky put fire through his veins. He stood there, staring down at the wet bar top. Tobacco smoke clouded against the reflectors. He listened to the murmur of voices, the clatter of a wagon in the street outside. Was this the way he was to spend the rest of his days? Alone. In a saloon with a glass in his hand. In a strange town, eyeing the girls, moving on. Talking tough, acting like a big bad curly wolf to let the locals know they couldn't get away with anything.

Hell. He was tired drifting, tired of talking tough, tired of convincing people in each new town that he was a little better than anyone around with a gun. Because it could end only one way. He would either face up to a better man or someone would shoot him in the back. You pushed and bullied your way just so long. He'd seen some of the good ones, the real good ones, and their blood was as red as the next man's and flowed as easily.

He caught a whiff of lilac and thought of Kate. Her warm smile, how she had looked in the dress. The curtains at the bedroom windows. Sheets on the bed. The good food and her sitting across from him at the table. . . .

A hand touched his arm. "Hello, Mister."

He turned and saw a girl smiling up at him. She had dark hair like Kate's, but the hair had no luster, and she was big through the hips.

He stared at her bare shoulders, the blouse cut revealingly low, the heavy flared skirt. Her hand tightened on his arm. "Come on, handsome."

He gave a short laugh. "Me—with this face?"

"I like your face."

Clay grunted in disgust. Fierro yelled something in Spanish to the girl. She shrugged and went outside.

"Where can I find a cattle buyer named Ruskin?" Clay asked Fierro.

He found Ed Ruskin smoking an evening cigar on the porch of the New Mexico Hotel. A short, well-fed man in a brown suit, Ruskin seemed delighted to see Clay.

After they shook hands, Clay took a chair on the porch and accepted a cigar. Ruskin said, "I need beef, Janner. I hear you've got some."

"Eight hundred head, more or less."

Ruskin brushed cigar ash off his vest. "I heard you and Alford had more than that." He sounded disappointed.

"The herd's split. I'm selling my half."

Ruskin chuckled. "That's the trouble with partnerships. They usually break up over a pretty woman. I hear that Nina Alford is a looker." He nudged Clay in the ribs. "Reckon you ought to know, eh?"

Clay said, "Too bad you weren't in the saloon a minute ago. I let it be known that I'd kill the man who talked against Mrs. Alford."

Ruskin seemed to sink down into his leather-padded chair. "I didn't mean anything. I—oh, you know how those stories get around."

"Just so we understand each other," Clay snapped. He shifted in his chair and the movement sent a twinge of pain along his ribs. "You'll take delivery of my herd here in Reeder Wells?"

"Now, wait a minute. Not so fast, Janner."

"I want to sell out and head for new territory."

Ruskin spread his pink hands. "I've got no crew for driving," he explained. "Only my shipping crew that will come in with the cars at Las Rosas in two weeks. I'll have to take delivery there. Now if we can look over your herd and talk business—"

Clay gripped the arms of his chair, thinking of Elkhart's forty-mile fence. Well, if Ruskin wouldn't take delivery here he'd have to make a drive himself. "Make an offer for the herd," he said.

"Sight unseen?" Ruskin shook his head. "That's no way to do business."

"I'm not making a drive to Las Rosas unless I know what to expect."

Ruskin drew thoughtfully on his cigar. Darkness lay over the town and the moon was beginning to show a yellow glow on the peaks of the Sabers. "I came here expecting to do business with Elkhart," Ruskin said heavily. "But he's

215

signed with somebody else. How much will your beef weigh out a head?"

"Eight hundred pounds, maybe."

"They won't average that if you drive 'em across the Sink," Ruskin said shrewdly.

"Who said I was going across the Sink?"

Ruskin sat up straighter in his chair. "You going through Elkhart's fence?"

Clay stared at him in the darkness. "How much if the herd averages out eight hundred?"

"Twenty dollars."

"You're a bandit," Clay said softly.

"Twenty-five, but not one red cent more."

Clay leaned close. "This country's gone to hell. It's a dry year and like you say Elkhart's signed with another outfit. And the basin ranchers are squirming on the hook, some wanting to sell out to Elkhart or pay toll or try driving across the Sink." He threw his cigar over the porch rail. "There won't be much beef coming out of here this season. But mine will be there." Clay paused a moment, then added, "You need beef to fulfill your contracts. How about it?"

It had been a gamble, but as Clay watched Ruskin's shadowed face he knew he had won.

"Twenty-seven-fifty a head. And I'll buy a drink to seal the bargain."

The cattle buyer started to hoist himself out of his chair, then seemed to freeze. Clay jerked around to see what had caught his attention. Russ Hagen, his right arm heavily bandaged and resting in a sling, came slowly up the steps of the hotel porch.

Clay got out of his chair. He eased farther back into the shadows. Hagen seemed to ignore him.

Ruskin stood up. "You're one of Elkhart's men," the cattle buyer said. "I saw you with him today. Now if Elkhart's sent you to make trouble, you forget it. I buy beef where I like—"

Hagen laughed. He extended his right hand a little in the sling. It was thickly covered with several layers of bandage. "Me make trouble with this arm? Hell, I just got a message. My boss said to tell you—"

Ordinarily, Clay's wits would have been sharper. But he was so deadly tired and his head still throbbed from the beating in the canyon. When Hagen first appeared he had been on his guard. But because Hagen showed no interest in him, patently ignoring him, he had relaxed.

And that had been his mistake.

Hagen had broken off speaking to Ruskin. He turned to Clay and pointed the bandaged hand at him. "Your luck's runnin' out of a leaky bucket, Janner!"

Even as Hagen spoke Clay realized the man's treacherous intent. He dived for the porch floor. Flame and explosion erupted from the bandaged hand. Two bullets ripped across the back of the padded chair he had been standing behind a split second ago.

In a desperate spasm of motion, Clay doubled up and rolled across the porch. Another bullet slashed into the flooring an inch from his head. Somebody was yelling from inside the hotel. A woman started to scream. And in that moment Clay got his gun out and struggled to his knees.

In the flare of a lamp above the hotel door he saw Hagen swinging the flaming bandages to cover him. Hagen was clenching his teeth, screaming from the pain of the burning cloth set afire by the powder. But the scream had rage in it too, rage and the resolve to finish what he had started.

Before he could trigger the revolver into Clay's face, Clay shot him. The bullet struck Hagen in the stomach, and as the big body started to bend, Clay's second bullet found hard bone in the chest. Hagen crashed through the porch rail to the walk below.

Men streamed out of the hotel. Fierro's cantina doors erupted and a crowd gathered fast.

Ruskin climbed shakily to his feet. The dive he had taken at the first shot had smashed his cigar against his lips but he still clenched the butt in his teeth. "My God," he muttered, and spat out the cigar. "I thought he had you, Janner. How did you do it?"

Numbly Clay clumped down to the walk. He got Hagen by the shoulder and rolled him over. He bent low and pulled aside the smouldering bandages. Hagen's fingers were still wrapped around a short-barreled pistol.

Clay got to his feet and said to the crowd, "The older the trick, the better it works. Because a man forgets."

Juan Fierro crossed himself.

Clay looked up at the porch. Dimly he made out the figure of Ruskin, surrounded by other guests of the hotel.

"Tell the sheriff how it happened," he said. "And remember, I'll see you in Las Rosas."

He got his horse and rode away from the

hotel. But from a corner of his eye he caught sight of Sheriff Lynden hurrying from the jail office to the scene of the shooting.

18

FOR two days Clay and his men sweated under the broiling sun to complete the gather. With Sam Lennox and two other hands it meant four riders to push nearly eight hundred steers northward. Clay couldn't thank Sam Lennox enough for riding with Kate and saving him from Elkhart and his men. Lennox just shrugged it off, telling Clay to watch his step. Joe Alford was still drunk, still talking trouble. But so far the redhead had not visited the holding grounds, and Clay was thankful for that. He had enough on his mind without tangling with Joe Alford. His main purpose now was to get out of New Mexico.

As he drove stubborn Chihuahuas out of the brush with the end of a saddle rope, he told himself again and again that this country had been a jinx to him. Both the country and the people in it. But no matter how he tried, he always felt a wrench when he thought of Kate.

After supper on the third night, Sam Lennox fell to telling some of the stories he'd heard about this new fencing material known as bobwire. "I hear a fella up north tried to make a corral of the stuff," the black-bearded rider confided, "but some of his hosses spooked and two of 'em got hung up on the wire and cut 'emselves to pieces." Lennox spat tobacco juice into the fire and wiped his beard on the back of his hand. "Funny thing. They say if a mule gets hung up in bobwire he'll stay put till somebody gets him loose. But not a hoss."

"Which only shows that mules have more sense than a lot of humans, myself included," Clay growled. And considering all the grief he'd experienced since he let Joe Alford talk him into coming here, he meant it.

When he rolled up in his blankets the night seemed to close in on him. He heard the restless herd, the soothing voices of the first trick guards. He felt edgy, and any foreign sound caused him to sit up and reach for his gun. But there was no sign of Elkhart or his men and this puzzled him. Surely by this time the rancher knew he intended taking the herd to Las Rosas, and would be out to stop him. For spite, if for no other reason.

He tried to sleep, but as always, the memory

of Kate French crowded into his mind. He felt more alone than at any other time in his life.

The next day they completed the gather. Just as they were about to start pushing the herd north, Clay caught sight of a dust cloud behind them. Elkhart, he thought, and drew his rifle and jacked in a shell. If there was trouble he meant to kill Elkhart and be done with it.

But instead of the Arrow crowd it was Kate French, riding point on a herd of about five hundred head. She came spurring up, a slim figure in denims and a man's shirt. Something tightened in Clay and he rode to meet her.

She regarded him levelly when they drew rein. "I'd like company on the drive to Las Rosas," she said. "Hope you won't mind if I tag along."

Her words caught him by surprise and for a moment he could think of nothing to say. She had nerve, this girl, and strength. It showed in her wide-spaced eyes, the good bone in her face, her firm full-lipped mouth. She showed no friendliness however. She acted as if she meant to treat this as strictly business.

"I'm not driving across the Sink," he told her.

"So I've heard."

He gave her a black scowl. "You'd go through Elkhart's fence with me?"

"Yes."

"You're the girl who didn't want trouble," he reminded her. "Who wanted to play the game safe. Even if it meant ruin."

"Maybe I've changed my mind," she said crisply, and lifted a hand to signal her men to hold her herd so they wouldn't mix with the Chihuahuas.

"I won't let you do it, Kate. Too much risk."

"I've seen trouble before in this country."

"And it killed your brother."

She bowed her dark head. "You don't have to remind me." She looked up. "I guess until men like Elkhart are put in their place we'll always need a man like my brother. Or a man like you."

Suddenly he felt warm and relaxed. "I'm glad you're still not mad."

"Why should I be mad?" She sounded indifferent. "You're fiddle-foot. You always will be. No woman could ever hold you and she'd be a fool to try." She reined her mount away from his. "Give me the signal when you're ready to start the drive. I'll trail along—"

And then Sam Lennox's shout drowned her out.

"Watch it, Clay! Joe Alford!"

Clay looked around, tense, and saw that Joe Alford had come up, the sounds of his approach hidden by the restless cattle. Alford drew rein a few feet away. He dismounted and put a hand to his horse to maintain his balance. He was red-eyed and a stubble of red whiskers blurred his jawline. He slapped his horse away and said thickly, "Get down, Clay."

A quick dryness parched Clay's throat. He swung down carefully.

"You're drunk, Joe," he said, trying to sound scornful. "Go home and tell Nina to get some black coffee into you. Then come back, if you're still set on it."

"You said the other day I got no guts. Maybe not. But I got the guts to face up to you. Pull that gun, Clay."

"Don't be a fool!"

"For once I'm goin' to fight!" He took a step toward Clay. "You ain't takin' Nina away from me!"

Clay spread his hands. "Elkhart lied."

Kate stepped down and came to Clay's side. He was surprised when he felt her soft arm slip

225

around his waist. "Clay isn't going to have two women, Joe," she said, and she kept her voice very level and calm because Alford was full of whisky and bewildered and choked with rage and he might start shooting. "Clay and I are going to be married. Now go home to Nina."

Clay didn't know who was more surprised— Joe Alford or himself. He looked down at Kate. She gave him a tight smile, then watched Alford again. The Chihuahuas at the mouth of a canyon stirred restlessly. Kate's men were standing up in their stirrups, trying to see what was going on. Sam Lennox stood a little to one side, holding a rifle.

Clay felt Kate tremble against him. He put his own arm about her waist. She clung to him tightly and her arm chafed the raw rope burns that circled his body.

"It's true, Joe," he managed to say. "Kate and me—"

"You're lyin'," Alford said.

"Go home to Nina," Kate said again.

For a moment the big redhead seemed utterly confused. Then he straightened up. "Get away from him, Kate. When I count to three I'm goin' for my gun. And he better go for his!"

Kate cried, "No!" but Alford began to count in a crazy screech.

"One, two—"

Clay lunged against Kate, knocking her to the ground. In the same movement he dived for Alford's legs. A gun roared. Something jerked the back of his shirt collar as he came in low, and then he crashed into Alford. They both went down, but Clay got up first. He kicked Alford's gun away. He stood glaring down at Alford, breathing heavily.

"You poor damn fool," he said.

Kate picked herself up and began brushing dust from her levis. She looked frightened. Some of the steers had started to bolt at the sound of the shot, but Lennox hit the saddle on the run and tore off to get them quieted.

Clay picked up Alford's gun. Alford wobbled and lurched up to his feet. He seemed dazed now.

Kate said, "Go home, Joe. Go home to Nina."

Alford didn't hear her. He pointed a thick, wavering finger at Clay. "Elkhart claimed you and Nina—"

"There's nothing between us, Joe."

"You said that before, when Russ Hagen seen you."

Clay hesitated, glanced at Kate, then said, "You won't have to worry about Hagen spreading any more stories. I killed him." He flicked another glance at Kate. She had gone white at the grim news.

Kate recovered her composure and said to Alford, "The day Elkhart says he found Nina and Clay together was the day I was there with them. Nina told Elkhart she wanted nothing to do with him. And to get even—to save his precious pride—Elkhart spread those dirty stories."

Clay started to jack the shells out of Alford's gun. "You don't have to do that," Alford said, and his voice was no longer thick.

Clay studied him a while, then handed over the loaded gun. Alford holstered the weapon, wiped a forearm across his mouth. He nodded at the two bunches of cattle and said, "A man can't make no money with cows in his own backyard. He's got to sell 'em." Then he caught up his horse and set it at a dead run toward Spade.

Clay stood woodenly, trying to remember just

what Kate had said and how she had said it. He felt a growing excitement. Yes, he remembered.

"You meant it?" he said. "About marrying me?"

She stepped away from him, suddenly cool and distant. "Alford was going to do something foolish. I lied to stop him. Nothing more."

The chill in her voice disturbed him. "You don't like it because I had to kill Hagen to save my own life."

She shrugged, but did not look at him. "That has nothing to do with it. I'd like to make the cattle drive with you to Las Rosas. But that's all I would like."

He wanted to argue with her, but decided against it. She was as unpredictable as the future, one moment apparently liking him, the next, hating him.

Because Kate knew the country well he had her draw a map on the ground with a pointed stick, showing Elkhart's property enclosed by the new fence. The most logical place to make a break through the fence, she explained, was on the old cattle trail at Juniper Crossing, almost due north from here. Clay picked a spot eight miles west, knowing that even with his full crew Elkhart could not hope to patrol the entire fence. It was a gamble, but his only chance. If they could make a towering rock known as Big Hat by midday tomorrow, they would be reasonably sure of success.

There would be a full moon tonight, and although Clay disliked pushing a herd in darkness, he knew it might give them a chance to get through Elkhart's fence and across his land before another night. He was gambling that Elkhart would expect trouble at those points where it would be easier to drive cattle, and leave the other crossing less heavily guarded.

They had been on the trail some hours when, shortly after moonrise, they reached the spot Clay had picked. Kate rode up and sat looking dolefully at the fence. Clay produced a pair of wire cutters and swung down.

"Here's your chance to turn back," he said.

"I'm game," she said, but he detected a note of anxiety beneath the boast.

Again he tried to get her to give up this foolhardy plan, but she told him if he wouldn't let her go along with his herd of Chihuahuas, she'd wait and cross later on her own.

"Might be better at that," Clay conceded. "Elkhart wouldn't likely make too much trouble for a woman."

"Don't be too sure," she said. "He hates me after I interfered the other day in the canyon."

Clay warned the men to be on their guard. They sat their saddles stiffly, holding rifles, peering off into the moon-swept flats that comprised Elkhart's formidable Arrow ranch. The cattle lowed, stomped the ground, not liking to be driven after dark. Clay cut the fence and with his saddle rope pulled aside the loose wires to clear the break. Black-bearded Sam Lennox quietly gave the order to push the combined herds through the fence. It was a grim business and Clay knew what each rider was thinking. Elkhart would treat a fence cutter the same way he'd deal with a rustler. There wasn't much to leave to the imagination.

Clay said to Kate, "Go on back, it's too risky." And when she refused again, he added, "You go home and I'll sell your herd in Las Rosas and send you the money. Or maybe you don't trust me."

"I trust you, Clay, and I'm going with you."

He extended his hand. She surprised him by leaning over in the saddle and taking it in her own. They looked at each other in the moonlight and he saw her teeth flash in a brief smile.

"It was all worth it," he said solemnly. "Everything. To find you."

Because he was caught up in the floss of a long-dead dream, he didn't hear the hoofbeats.

"Somebody's coming," Kate whispered.

He reined off, drawing his rifle. Not fifty yards away, two riders pulled up their horses and looked at the cattle streaming through the break in the fence. Then they wheeled and went pounding back over their own trail at a dead run.

Shouting at Lennox to keep the cattle moving, Clay dug in the spurs and started after them. Those two riders must have been sent out by Elkhart to patrol a section of the fence. Once they reported their findings, the whole Arrow crew would take the warpath.

Recklessly Clay kept his horse at a gallop, ignoring the danger of riding full tilt over the uneven ground in the moonlight. But the roan had speed and wind and quick sure feet. At first Clay thought he would never be able to overtake them. Then he began to gain. Wind stung his eyes.

In one way the moonlight was a blessing, in another, a curse. For there were two of them and he was clearly silhouetted.

One of the riders ahead turned in the saddle. A red eye winked at him. He heard the angry whine of metal beside his head, then the crash of a rifle. He looped the reins loosely over the saddle-horn, lifted his own rifle and took quick aim. As he squeezed off a shot he saw another red dot and then felt the lethal whip of air across his face. He fired again. One of the shadows ahead slid off a horse and into deeper shadows. He came thundering up, passed a riderless horse and something that thrashed weakly upon the ground.

He was closing in on the second man when the rider's horse stumbled. The man fought to keep his saddle, then went cartwheeling into the brush.

Reining in, Clay came up slowly, holding his rifle on the man. The rider rolled over and climbed to his feet, hands lifted. "Don't shoot, Janner," he said. "Reckon you don't remember me—Bob Bailey. Fella that was drivin' the wagon load of wire the day your cows stampeded."

Bailey was trembling, and his mouth hung open so that Clay could see his teeth through the tangle of brown beard. He acted as if he expected to be shot. "Where's Elkhart?" Clay demanded, dismounting and drawing the man's gun.

"He's got a camp 'bout ten mile east," Bailey said, watching Clay's rifle. "He's got the crew strung out along the whole fence. If there's trouble the one that spots it is supposed to round up the other boys. You sure crossed him up by makin' your drive at night. Only a fool would do that. Them cows are liable to run."

"If they do, they'll run toward Las Rosas. You're riding with us."

Bailey's horse, recovered from the fall, stood some distance away. Clay caught it and led the animal back to Bailey. As they started back Clay saw that clouds were whipping in from the north, screening the peaks of the Sabers. If the night turned black it could hamper the drive.

When they reached the spot where Clay had shot Bailey's companion, they found the man passed out. Clay's bullet had smashed into his right shoulder. They got the man into the saddle and Bailey, riding alongside, held him there.

"You got to know this, Janner," Bailey said, when they were moving toward the herd. "I got no love for Elkhart. I draw his pay but I ain't goin' to risk my neck for the likes of him." He turned in the saddle. "He says he'll hang anybody that cuts his fence."

"That might take some doing," Clay snapped, but it didn't take away the chill brought by Bailey's words.

When they caught up with the herd Kate smiled her relief. Clay put Bailey to work, helping push the herd, but he warned the men to keep an eye on him. The wounded man— Bert Collins—had regained consciousness. Sam Lennox bound up his shoulder. The rider managed to stay in the saddle of one of the extra horses, but that was about all.

Tense and weary, they drew up as light touched the eastern horizon, and ate jerky and cold biscuits. Clay was disappointed to see that although they were several miles from the fence they still had not reached Big Hat. The rock was still ahead of them.

As they drove the tired, balky herd north, Clay kept riding back to the drag, bandanna over his nose to screen out the dust, scanning their backtrail. Any man with the eye of a pigeon could see this funnel of dust. He expected Arrow to come at them any minute. The deeper they got into Elkhart's land, the more he cursed himself for allowing Kate to accompany him on this mad venture. But if she felt any fear she didn't show it. She did a man's work in the saddle, flicking the end of her saddle rope on the hides of steers trying to cut away from the herd, going after strays.

Two hours after daylight he heard the crackle of distant gunfire. He drew rein, listening. Kate watched him anxiously through the dust. Another burst of fire reached him and he guessed the position to be somewhere around Juniper Crossing. Some poor fool trying to get through the fence at the obvious crossing, where Elkhart was bound to be waiting. Who was it? Bogarth? Not likely. Maybe Leo Reese or Shanley.

He had a sudden urge to take his men and ride to the aid of this unfortunate. But he knew this wasn't possible. He owed something to Kate. He couldn't just ride off. And besides, he told himself angrily, if the pool had stuck together, they could have all broken through the fence at the same time. There'd have been a war, sure, but it was better than knuckling under to Elkhart, paying toll or driving across the Sink.

Not that he had made any great show of it, he told himself. The Chihuahuas were still scrawny. The sparse Spade grass had not put any weight on them, and by the time they made this fast drive they would weigh in even less. Ruskin would take one look at them and cut his price, and Clay couldn't blame him.

An hour later he almost reeled with shock when Nina Alford, her blonde hair loose about her shoulders, come pounding up on a spent horse. Clay wheeled away from the herd and managed to catch Nina just as she fainted dead away. As he lowered her to the ground, Kate rode up and dropped down at his side.

19

THE herd milled and the riders gathered to see what the Alford woman's presence meant. Clay gave Nina a drink from his canteen. Her eyes opened. She looked wildly around, then clutched his hands.

"Elkhart's got Joe," she whispered hoarsely. "He's going to hang him unless—"

"Unless what?"

"Unless you give yourself up, Clay."

Clay scowled. "Elkhart knew where to send you to find me?" he demanded. And when the blonde head nodded, he said, "Why doesn't he jump us then?"

"He hasn't enough men," Nina explained breathlessly. "His crew is scattered along the fence." She whimpered once. "But he can still hang Joe."

Clay got up slowly. The palms of his hands were moist. "How'd Joe get himself into this mess?" he asked.

"Last night he insisted on starting out with about a hundred head of cattle," Nina explained in a dead voice. "He said if you could do it so could he. I came with him because he was still drunk." She pushed a trembling hand across her forehead. "Elkhart disarmed the crew Joe had with him and sent them back across the fence. Then he told me I could save Joe's life if I found you—and got you to come back." She bit her lip. "Oh, Clay, what are we going to do? I don't want Joe hurt. I—love him, Clay. But it isn't right to ask you to save him."

Clay climbed heavily into the saddle. Kate said, "Don't, Clay. Don't try to do it alone!"

"Keep the herd moving—fast," he ordered. "I didn't rot in a Mex prison to come up here and turn my profit over to Byrd Elkhart."

Kate beat her hands together. "Is that all you care about? Just profit?"

"Do what I told you!" he yelled.

Sam Lennox reined in beside him. "I'll go with you, Clay."

Clay nodded. "A bonus for this, Sam. You'll earn it."

"The hell with that, boss. You saved my neck in the stampede. I'm not goin' for the money."

"And you saved my neck in the canyon." They were riding stirrup to stirrup. "You'll still get that bonus."

As they rode Clay tried to set himself straight on the baffling subject of Joe Alford. Crazy damn fool, Joe. Drunk and reckless. Exposing not only himself to danger, but his wife and his friends. Friend, though. Was he really Joe's friend? How much did he owe Joe Alford? Their association these past months had brought them both nothing but trouble.

Yet he kept stubbornly on, and within a few miles he caught the flash of sunlight on glass. Somebody tracking their approach through field glasses. Well, the hell with it. There was no use in trying to sneak up on them.

"Let's come at 'em from two sides," Clay said. "If things get too rough, hightail it. Get back to the herd and watch out for Kate French. I'll try and get Joe out of this. And if I don't—"

Lennox shot him a sidelong glance. "First time I ever knew you to have any doubts, Clay."

"Maybe I don't show it, but you'd be surprised how much mush a man has in his guts at times."

"You ain't the only one, Clay. Me too."

"You can still keep out of it, Sam."

"You don't let a man hang if you can help

240

it," Lennox said soberly. He wheeled away from Clay and rode east so as to come up on Elkhart's camp from the opposite direction.

Finally Clay reached the crest of a hill. He drew rein and saw Elkhart resting on a deadfall in the center of a small basin that was Juniper Crossing. A dry creek bed followed the cut fence for a hundred yards, then veered south into the undergrowth.

Elkhart lifted a lazy hand in greeting to Clay. So far as Clay could tell, Elkhart had only two men with him. One of them held three horses. The second stood beside Joe Alford's buckskin horse. Alford sat the saddle, with hands roped behind his back and a noose around his neck. Clay's breath caught in his throat when he saw that the end of the rope had been played out over a cottonwood limb and tied to the trunk of the tree. If that buckskin horse made one wrong move Joe Alford would be hanging by his neck.

Carefully, rifle in hand, Clay moved his horse down the slope. Elkhart's confidence bothered him. The man actually seemed to be enjoying himself. Fifty feet away from Joe Alford, Clay reined in.

Elkhart got slowly to his feet, stretched, then

said, "I've sent word to the rest of my crew to head this way."

"So."

"Two of my boys are missing or we'd have corraled my crew sooner than this. Those two were supposed to do the patrolling. Don't suppose you know anything about them disappearing, do you, Janner?"

"Nina Alford said you wanted me," Clay said. "I'm here."

Elkhart looked him over. "You've been a tough opponent, Janner. I could ride your bunch down and shoot you to pieces. But you've cost me a lot and I'm going to do it differently. I want to see you sweat." He glanced at his two men, one holding the horses, the other at the rump of the buckskin horse that held Joe Alford. "I want your herd for damages, Janner."

Clay gave a short laugh to mask his uneasiness. "Damages for what?"

"You trespassed. You cut my fence. Sign over your herd to me and put yourself in my hands so I can turn you over to the sheriff. Do that and I'll let Alford go."

"Don't listen to him, Clay," Joe Alford said, but sweat was running down his face in rivulets.

242

Elkhart turned his head slightly and told him to shut up.

"Janner, if you try any of your tricks—and you've got a lot of them I admit—I'll give Lew a signal." He indicated the slight, tense, bowlegged man who stood beside the buckskin. "Lew will slap that horse out from under your friend. Alford won't stand a chance. There's enough slack in that rope to snap his neck."

Clay looked at Alford. The sign of doom was on him.

Elkhart laughed quietly. "See what I mean by doing this my way? You're beginning to sweat too, Janner."

And Clay knew he was right. His armpits were wet and moisture had gathered on his forehead and a drop of it stung his eye. He licked his dry lips and gauged the distance to that slender strand of hemp leading from Alford's neck to the cottonwood limb. The rope was new, yellow and unstained. He could see it clearly, but it was such a small target. The rifle felt slick in his hands. Elkhart was enjoying this.

"Drop your gun, Janner." Elkhart turned and pointed to Sam Lennox, who had ridden to a hogback directly south of the camp and sat

243

his saddle, unmoving. "Tell your rider to drop his gun. Then you come down here—with your hands up. Write an order to your men to turn the herd over to me. Then I'll see that Alford stays alive."

Clay pretended to deliberate, but from a corner of his eye he made his calculations. With a sort of frozen desperation he gauged the wind and the drop from his own higher elevation down to Alford.

Elkhart said, "I want to see just how deep this friendship is. Are you going to save Alford? Or are you going to ride out. I'll let you go if you want."

Clay showed his teeth. "You're a liar. If I play your game you'll hang me along with Alford."

Elkhart shook his head. "You'll be turned over to the sheriff. This much I promise. I give my word."

"Your word!" Clay mocked him arrogantly, but his heart was thundering.

"Better make up your mind. The buckskin is getting restless."

Clay seemed to sag. "All right," he said, and swung down, still holding his rifle.

"Smart," Elkhart said. "You've got no choice

unless you want to see Alford hang. And if you figure to put a bullet in me, it'll be the same as putting one in Alford. Either way he'll be dead."

Clay licked his lips again. The bowlegged man called Lew had removed his hat and stood ready to slap the buckskin from under Alford if Elkhart gave the signal. He strained his ears, listening for sounds of Elkhart's riders, answering the summons of their employer.

"Drop that rifle," Elkhart said again. "Quick."

Clay made as if to fling it into the brush. Then he pivoted, flung up the weapon and sighted. He heard Elkhart's shout. The bowlegged rider slapped the buckskin with his hat. With a snort the animal bolted away from the tree just as Clay fired. He saw the slender rope jerk and fray as if cut part way through with a knife. Alford swayed in the saddle, trying desperately to keep his balance. The rope whipped tight, almost yanking Alford out of the saddle. And then it parted with an audible twang.

Clay wheeled to line the rifle on Elkhart. He heard a burst of firing and something slammed into him. The blow knocked him to the ground.

As he lay there, dazed, he saw Lew take a few staggering steps and collapse. There was more firing, a roar of hoofbeats, then silence.

After his head cleared, Clay got to his feet. He saw Sam Lennox wheel his horse and come spurring back. "I winged that fella with Elkhart. Guess Elkhart figured the game was too rough." Lennox grinned hugely through his beard.

"Go after Alford!" Clay shouted, and Lennox spurred away again.

Clay looked down. His left sleeve was stained. He managed to clench his fingers, so he knew that no tendons had been cut. It was just a flesh wound, but the heavy caliber slug had struck him at such an angle that it knocked him off his feet.

From the distance came the crash of a rifle and Clay got a glimpse of Elkhart on a knoll some hundred yards away. Before Clay reached his horse, Elkhart spurred out of sight. Clay wondered who Elkhart was shooting at. The bullet had not been aimed at him. He rode past the bowlegged Lew, who was writhing on the ground from a thigh wound, and pushed on. He rode into a brushy draw and there he saw Alford's buckskin with Alford aboard, his hands still tied. A short distance away Sam Lennox lay face down in the dirt.

"Elkhart got him just as he was comin' to cut me loose," Alford said.

Clay dismounted and kneeled beside Lennox and his stomach churned. There was nothing he could do for Sam Lennox now. He couldn't even bury him decently.

"Let's go after Elkhart!" Alford shouted. "The sonofabitch oughta be shot for this!"

Clay managed to get back into the saddle. He rode close and thumbed his clasp knife open and cut Alford's bonds.

"No time to go after Elkhart," Clay said. "Sam's done for but there's Kate and Nina. We've got to get them out of Elkhart's reach."

"Yeah," Alford said dully. "If Elkhart's crew gets here we're all done for."

They lined their horses north. "You shouldn't have risked your neck comin' after me," Joe Alford said.

Clay gave him a faint grin. He said, "You're my partner, Joe," and suddenly he knew that somewhere in this world a man had to put down his roots. All his neighbors couldn't be strong and bravely confident of coping with any crisis. There had to be some who were just likable, some whom you'd have to help once in a while. Men like Joe Alford. The world wasn't perfect, and Clay knew that had been his failing. Hunting for perfection in land and in women. Free grass in Montana where there might be worse obstacles than barbed wire. And Kate . . . She had spirit and might be hard to handle. But where could a man do better?

Sam Lennox had given his life to help the man who had pulled him out from under a raging stampede. Sam would want him to make his sacrifice count, right here where the trail ended naturally for Clay Janner, whether he lived or died.

After they had gone several miles, Joe Alford said glumly, "It was the whisky that made me brave enough to cut Elkhart's fence."

"And he was waiting for you," Clay said. "You're lucky he didn't hang you right off."

"Nina bein' with me was the only thing that stopped him. He figured it would be funny to send her after you. Poetic justice, he called it."

Sometime later they heard a roar of hoofs. They hid in the junipers and saw a group of riders spurring in the direction of the fence. Elkhart's men. They started out again. Clay felt light in the head. His arm throbbed.

Alford said, "Reckon it was me that let Elkhart know you'd cut his fence. I bragged that if anybody got through it'd be you. I figured you and Kate would be across his range by this time."

Clay shifted his left arm to ease it. "Trailing a herd at night is slow," he said, and Alford noticed his bloodied shirtsleeve for the first time.

"Clay, you been hit."

"Yeah."

"We better stop and bandage—"

"We better get out of here," Clay corrected. "It won't take Elkhart long to round up his men. When he does they'll be after us."

Finally they caught up with the herd. The cattle were being pushed hard. Clay passed on the details of the fight while Kate bandaged his wound. When she finished she kissed him lightly on the lips, and then they rode after the herd. On the move, Clay told his men about Sam Lennox.

"You boys will get the bonus I promised Sam," he said. Near nightfall Kate announced that they were now off Elkhart's range. They slowed their pace and watered the herd at a half-dry stream. Then they pushed on. Clay scouted their back-trail, expecting to see Elkhart's men riding to cut them off from Las Rosas. He was surprised when it didn't happen. His arm pained and he felt a little sick from losing so much blood.

When at last they camped, Joe Alford sat by the fire, one arm about Nina's waist. "I'm stayin' put from now on, Clay. If you was to come up with the best gun-running deal in the world, I'd turn you down."

"Don't worry," Clay said with a faint smile. "It'd take more than guns to get me away from here."

"Sometimes I think I've had troubles," Nina said quietly. "But what if I'd married a man like Byrd Elkhart."

"I guess none of us knew what he really was," Kate said, and glanced tensely off into the darkness. "Why hasn't he hit us? What is he waiting for?"

"He's got an ace up his sleeve, you can be sure of that," Clay said grimly. "At least we won't have to worry about Elkhart's bought-and-paid-for sheriff in Las Rosas."

"That's where you're wrong, Clay," Kate

said with a catch in her voice. "This is a big county. Las Rosas is the northern boundary."

Clay groaned silently. So far they had been lucky. But how long could it last?

20

SEVERAL days later, Clay got his first glimpse of Las Rosas. It was a comparatively new town; false-fronted buildings of rough, unpainted lumber lined both sides of the main street. Beyond some warehouses lay the shining tracks of the railroad. At the west end of town were a dozen or more big cattle pens. They drove the herd to one of the empty pens. Just as Clay shut the gate he saw a familiar figure riding toward them: Sheriff Bert Lynden, long legs hugging the barrel of a paint horse.

Lynden swung down, his every gesture indicating an intense dislike for Clay Janner. "This here's a court order," Lynden said, handing Clay a legal-looking document. "You don't sell that herd till you satisfy a judgment for damages."

Clay shoved the paper in his pocket. "So Elkhart's in town," he said.

"Not yet, but I expect him any time. He sent a rider to tell his lawyer to start this action. And you better mind that court order or you'll find yourself in jail." He nodded at Kate. "That includes your cows too, Miss French. You both cut Elkhart's barb wire and trespassed on his land and tromped his waterholes and—"

"Get out of here," Clay said, "before I lose my temper."

The sheriff glared at him, but then he rode back toward the center of town.

"Now what do we do?" Kate asked dispiritedly.

"We hire a lawyer," Clay said. "He wants a court fight. He's going to get it." He caught her by the arms. "Kate, this is our chance, and Elkhart's given it to us. We'll bring his fence out into the open. No judge can do anything but rule in our favor. Elkhart will be forced to tear it down."

"But—"

"It's illegal, Kate. Elkhart knows it as well as anybody else. He's good and mad on account of Nina. And he's trying to bluff. But sometimes when a man lets his temper get the best of him he does some foolish things. This is one of them." He slapped at the pocket holding the court order.

He told Kate to take Nina and go uptown and shop. Then he suggested that Alford stay with the herd, and he turned Bailey and his wounded companion loose.

Uptown Clay found Ed Ruskin in the bar of the Frontier House. The cattle buyer was in a sour mood, having learned of the restraining order.

"I can use that beef right now, Janner," Ruskin said dolefully. "The cars are ordered. But we can't move as long as Elkhart's got the sheriff on his side."

"We'll see about that," Clay said. He had a glass in hand that Ruskin had filled from his bottle. The barroom was crowded. With the coming of the railroad Las Rosas was booming.

As Clay lifted his glass he glanced through the dirty saloon window and saw Byrd Elkhart and Lon Perry on the opposite side of the street. The tall, heavy-set rancher was talking to his yellow-haired foreman. After a minute or so Perry nodded and disappeared in the crowd. Elkhart came toward the saloon.

Ruskin was saying, "If Elkhart keeps up these tactics I'll be out of business around here."

"Here he comes now," Clay said. "Maybe I can show him the error of his ways. It would be the mistake of his life to try and take us to court."

Elkhart entered the saloon, then stopped when he saw Clay. "You ready to settle up for the damage you did my property?" he demanded.

There was an instant silence in the room.

Clay walked slowly toward the man, halting a few feet away. "That fence of yours will never stand up in court, Elkhart."

"I've got enough money to see this case drag on for a year or more. By that time you'll be broke."

Clay jerked a thumb at Ruskin. "This cattle buyer has a stake in this country, along with a lot of other people. If you try and force that judgment on me, Ruskin might go to the Territorial governor—"

"I don't scare worth a damn," Elkhart muttered, but he gave Ruskin a wary glance.

"And I'll do that," Ruskin said boldly. "Competition is good for business. And my company can't do business in a county if a man like you tries to hog it all. You can just about set your own terms for beef on this range. And it's no good that way."

Elkhart scowled. He seemed a little shaken,

evidently not having counted on Ruskin turning on him. He started to say something, but didn't. His yellow-brown eyes smoldered.

Clay noticed Sheriff Bert Lynden at the edge of the crowd, and decided to play it to the hilt.

"This country is growing and maybe next election time Bert Lynden will have to count votes from the little outfits, as well as the big." Clay paused to let that sink in, and Lynden listened with his mouth open. "If he wants to wear that badge another term he'd better quit catering to men like you and do an honest job."

"Who says I ain't honest!" Lynden roared, pushing his way forward.

Before Clay could answer, half a dozen men in the crowd spoke up. "You been Elkhart's man all along, Sheriff. If that ain't bein' dishonest I don't know what is."

Lynden turned red in the face, made a strangling noise, then wheeled abruptly and stormed out of the Frontier House. Somebody laughed at his back, but the sheriff didn't turn around.

Elkhart's face was white. "You move that herd, Janner, and you'll be in jail."

He started toward the door, and at that moment a man burst into the building—a

256

slightly built, freckle-faced man in range clothes. He was covered with dust and patches of sweat showed on his shirt. He looked as if he had traveled a great distance, fast.

One of the Arrow men, Clay guessed, and watched tensely as the rider signaled to Elkhart and whispered something in his ear. Elkhart turned, a thin smile of triumph on his lips.

"I got you up short this time, Janner," he said. "Real short!" He came toward Clay, and men stepped aside to give him room. "I've had men lookin' for an old reprobate named Charlie Snow. Well, they found him at last. Snow's in the Reeder Wells jail. Held as a material witness. And Charlie Snow has told what he did with the body of Baldy Renson. You paid Snow to hide Renson's body—"

"You're a liar!"

"Careful, Janner." Elkhart was grinning. "You shot Baldy. My rider. Shot him inside my property line. Lon Perry and two more of my boys saw you do it. But by the time you drove 'em off with some fancy rifle fire, you'd hid Baldy's body and—"

Elkhart was reaching for his gun. Clay beat him to it. There was a collective gasp of surprise in the room, a frantic shuffling of feet as men fought to get out of the way. Behind the bar a bartender dropped a bottle in his excitement.

Clay thumbed back the hammer of his revolver. "You know that's a lie," he said thinly, trying not to show the fear riding him. "The truth isn't in you. Sure I killed Renson. But only when he tried to shoot me in the back —on your orders!"

Elkhart crouched slightly, hands away from his body. He lifted his gaze from Clay's gun. "You're going back to Reeder Wells and stand trial, Mr. Janner," he said slowly. "You're going to hang for this. Understand?"

He turned his back on the gun and walked out of the saloon. After he cleared the door, Ruskin said, "I don't know anything about this Renson business. But if I were you I'd clear out, Janner. If Elkhart hasn't got a warrant for you, he'll get one damn quick."

Clay holstered his gun. He saw everybody looking at him. It was one thing to buck a man like Elkhart because of a barbed wire fence. It was something else again to be accused of murder.

The bartender said in a loud voice, "I'd be obliged if you step outside, Mister. I don't want this place shot up."

Clay went out and stood under the saloon's overhang. Here the blinding sun could not reach. He watched the passers-by, women and townsmen and ranchers, all hurrying about their business. Kate was somewhere in this town. If he ran now he would never see her again. A month, a week ago he would have climbed on his horse and headed for the badlands, chalking this adventure up to a bad run of the cards. Looking for new fields. But now . . .

He felt empty and alone. With Elkhart's witnesses and Elkhart's judge and jury they would walk him to the gallows as sure as the sun rose in the morning.

Joe Alford came along the walk. "Hey, Clay, I—"

"I thought I told you to stay with the herd!" Clay snarled.

The big redhead just grinned at him. "Kate sent me to tell you the good news. She found a lawyer and he's takin' the case. He says Elkhart ain't got the chance of an icicle in July. He says—"

Clay stomped his boot heel on the board walk. "Listen, Joe, things are a lot more serious."

"My God, Clay, what's the matter?"

"I want you to look after Kate. I—"

From the corner of his eye he saw Elkhart appear on the opposite side of the street. Elkhart stopped in front of a drygoods store. He was holding a rifle. Coming along the center of the street was the slender, yellow-haired Lon Perry. And on Perry's shirt, Clay saw a badge.

He said, "Get out of here, Joe," and tried to push the big redhead aside.

Alford didn't budge. He turned and saw Perry. "So Bert Lynden pinned a badge on him. What's this mean, Clay?"

"It means I've got about ten seconds to either give myself up or shoot my way out."

21

A FROTHY layer of clouds lay against the mountains behind the town. A breeze had come up, blowing hot off the Sink. Despite the heat, Clay felt a cold gnawing fear in his stomach. He glanced to the south end of town where the herd was penned. He thought of Kate. To come this far and lose it all to a man like Elkhart. God.

He swiveled his head, expecting to see Sheriff Bert Lynden somewhere near Elkhart and Perry. There was no sign of the lawman. And then Clay knew why. In this showdown Lynden had delegated his authority to Lon Perry. Lynden was not only an inefficient sheriff; he was a coward, letting someone else run the risk of a gunfight.

Elkhart and Perry were standing still now, one on the walk, one in the street, watching him. Some of the crowd sensed the tension. The walks miraculously cleared. There were frightened squeals from women as they herded their children to safety.

Ed Ruskin's voice reached Clay. "Looks like Elkhart's goin' to make you sweat for this one, Janner. Perry's got a badge. If you shoot him now you'll really be up against the law and no foolin'. Back off, Janner. You still got time."

Clay shifted his gaze, saw the small, plump cattle buyer in the doorway of the Frontier House. He shook his head at the man and turned to look again at Elkhart and Perry.

"I'm with you, Clay," Joe Alford said at his elbow. He sounded scared but grimly determined. "I've got that cat off my back, Clay."

"You're no hand with a gun, Joe. Keep out of it. You've got a wife to think of."

"She'd hate me sure if I didn't side you. I'd hate myself—"

Elkhart began edging along the walk, cradling his rifle. "Unbuckle your gunbelt, Janner," he ordered, and Lon Perry started to pace slowly forward.

At the same instant Clay spied Nina and Kate French hurrying across the street. "Keep back!" he shouted, and saw Elkhart raise his rifle.

Clay dug for his gun just as Kate seized Nina by a wrist and dragged her out of the line of fire. And Clay sensed movement beside him and

262

knew Alford was drawing with him. He felt a flash of pride for Joe and also a vast fear. There was a crash of guns. An orange-red streak of flame leaped from Elkhart's rifle and Alford, spinning, slumped against Clay, spoiling his aim. Clay's bullet whined off a metal sign above the drygoods store.

Clay leaped aside and saw Joe Alford drop to the edge of the walk.

Lon Perry yelled, "I'm arresting you, Janner!"

"The hell you are!" Clay swung his gun and the movement brought a stab of pain to his left arm. The wound slowed him perceptibly and he knew he could never get set before Elkhart caught him in a crossfire.

He was aware of Nina screaming, of men in the saloon ducking below the window. He fired, but Perry had already lined his gun and he felt a savage blow at his right leg. He fell into the street, rolled over, still holding his gun. He heard a roar behind him and saw Elkhart stumble back against a building front. Elkhart dropped his rifle and pitched forward across the walk.

Lon Perry risked a glance at Elkhart, seemed to hesitate, then began firing. Clay squeezed off a shot, but Perry still kept coming. Perry had lost his hat. His face was slick with sweat, his yellow hair loose about his face. Desperately Clay flung himself aside as a bullet struck the ground, peppering his neck with grit.

As he came to a sitting position he fired the gun as fast as he could lift the hammer and drop it. At each shot Perry wavered. But still he came on, staggering drunkenly now. Clay watched him, numbly knowing his own gun was empty. If Perry had one more bullet and had the strength to lift the gun for a final shot, it was all over.

And then Perry's legs seemed to collapse. He folded up in the street and didn't move.

For what seemed like an age Clay just sat there letting the tension drain out of him. He watched the crowd gathering but ignored the jumbled, shouted questions. Then Kate was kneeling beside him, weeping.

All he could say was, "Joe, is he—"

"He shot Elkhart. He was lying face down and somehow he managed to shoot—" Kate buried her head against his shoulder. "Oh, Clay, I was so scared."

Clay watched some men pick up Joe Alford

and carry him down the street. After a minute or so they picked him up too.

There was a doctor's office above the dry-goods store, and there the doctor removed a bullet from Clay's leg. For several hours they did not know whether Alford would make it. But at last the doctor gave his assurance that he would pull through.

A crowd kept milling in the street and in the hallways outside the doctor's office, all gabbing about the gunfight. Elkhart was dead, shot between the eyes by a bullet from Joe Alford's gun. Lon Perry lived for an hour. Before he died he confessed that Elkhart had paid Baldy Renson to ambush Clay Janner. And Renson probably got caught in his own trap. So they all said, over and over again.

Sheriff Bert Lynden came along the hall, and the crowd fell silent. In the doorway of the doctor's office Lynden removed his hat and looked in at Clay, and at Kate, and at Joe Alford, who was propped up in a cot with Nina in a chair beside him.

"I just want you to know," the sheriff said, clearing his throat, "that I didn't swear in Perry as a deputy. He stole that badge from me and pinned it on."

"And you let him," Clay said.

"He threatened me," Lynden said.

Nobody said anything at all after that, and the sheriff turned around slowly and went back along the hall. He was through and he knew it.

Kate leaned close to Clay. "Don't be a fiddle-foot any more. Please stay and help me run KJ."

"It's your ranch," Clay said, and looked across the room at Nina and Alford, who were talking earnestly. "Joe married a woman with a ranch. It just doesn't work out."

"But they're going to get along now," Kate said.

"I'll stay if you let me buy a half interest in KJ. Maybe when I sell the herd it won't be enough. But one of these days I'll have the cash and—"

"You're going to be only a partner?" Kate said, drawing back.

He gave her a faint smile. "Anything the matter with marrying your partner?"

According to Kate, there wasn't.